# The Art of
# Featherwork
## in Old Hawai'i

*This book is for Patches, for Fredda
and for my mother – three women
of extraordinary quality.*

Copyright © 1985 by John Dominis Holt

Library of Congress Cataloging in Publication Data Number
has been applied for.

Typography by Innovative Media Inc., Honolulu

Printed in Hong Kong by Toppan Printing (HK) Ltd in
cooperation with Emphasis International (HK) Ltd

Designed by Leonard Lueras and Steve Shrader
Frontispiece and other illustrations by Denise DeVone

ISBN: 0-914916-68-8
The Art of Featherwork in Old Hawai'i

Published by:
TOPGALLANT PUBLISHING CO., LTD
Honolulu, Hawai'i 96813

# The Art of
# *Featherwork*
## in Old Hawai'i

John Dominis Holt

Published by Topgallant Publishing Co., Ltd.
First Edition 1985

These splendid feather garments are on exhibit in The National Museum of Denmark, Copenhagen. Although the model is not Hawaiian, he has the height and dignity to display handsomely these examples of old Hawaiian featherwork. The idea here is well intended and has resulted in the finest display there is of a high chief of Hawai'i wearing full regalia.

# Contents

# Preface

THE PURPOSE OF THIS BOOK is to describe in detail various aspects of Hawaiian featherwork. Each garment or object will be discussed in regard to its artistic design and appearance, its symbolic significance, the genealogical and heraldic implications in its design, and the practical uses and historic importance of these extraordinary creations. Lastly, I will comment on the whereabouts of each garment or ornament described.

There is very little documentation by Hawaiians about the subject of Hawaiian featherwork. I have relied upon family history, legends, chants and oral histories of older Hawaiians, as well as documented sources. My Hawaiian heritage as a descendent of some of the chiefs of old Hawai'i gives me a strange spiritual desire, almost a mandate, to share my thoughts with you. There is a strong mystical element in these feather capes and cloaks, and other featherworks. Each has a different design and message about 'aumakua, 'ohana and spirituality.

I am struck over and over again by the mystery locked into these antiquated feather garments. I keep going back to look at them wherever they are in the world's museums. There is always something more to see. They tease the imagination and tantalize that sense of wonderment that is now lost to us in the way of meaning and in the high style of metaphor locked into those garments made by Hawaiian men and women many years ago—among them some of my ancestors. Underlying what is seen in what remains of Hawaiian featherwork is a strong leitmotif of spirituality. Forms, shapes and colors result in designs that are wonderfully suggestive of cosmic powers. We are constantly taken by the sight of these designs to the deeper layers of human survival impulses where veneration of unseen power, respect for the old gods and a true belief in the magic that lies at the edges of reality was profoundly established within the center of everyday life.

I am linked to these feather objects by virtue of lineage. I am born to this link. They speak to me with other stimuli. The drumbeat and the chant reach into me to touch deepest spiritual feelings. I am taken with the idea that, in wearing their capes and cloaks, the old Hawaiians got just a little closer to the eternal, to the unending realm of poetry and song in which the visible recedes into the background, and into simple routines of daily existence framed by imaginations and souls nourished by the singing of the skies.

—J.D.H.

*(Opposite page) In this portrait by John Hayter, the high chief Boki Kama-uleule and his wife, the high chiefess Kuini Liliha, were both members of the royal strain of Maui, the Pi'ilani. Here, Boki is wearing a cloak and helmet peculiar in style to Maui. Liliha is wearing a thick band of mamo feathers. Around her neck she is wearing a niho palaoa.*
*— Courtesy of the Bernice Pauahi Bishop Museum*

*(Following pages) This painting by Titian Peale was made during a visit to Hawai'i in 1846. It depicts a scene at Halema'uma'u Crater of a group of chiefs and kahunas, some wearing feather garments. The sitting figures in white are probably of the pi'o rank, the highest rank of Hawaiian society.*
*—Courtesy of the Bernice Pauahi Bishop Museum*

# First Encounters

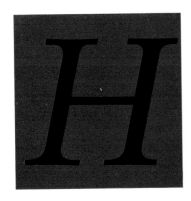

ISTORY'S FIRST RECORDED OBSERVATIONS of Hawaiian featherwork were made in January 1778 by Captain James Cook and some of the men who made up the ships' companies on his third and last voyage of exploration. It was on the island of Kaua'i where they first saw chiefs splendidly draped in their *'ahu'ula* and *mahiole*, their capes, cloaks and helmets. The royal family of Kaua'i, headed by Queen Kamakahelei, visited both the *Resolution* and the *Discovery*.

> Karanatoa brother to Teeave came on board the Ship this morning with a man carrying an enormous fly flap before him on his Shoulder,[1] . . . Soon after Tamataherei[2] accompanied by her husband Ta-eoh . . . paid us a Visit . . . they had not been long on board before the appearance of Too-mahana[3] was announced to us by the Indians on board the Ship & in the Canoes all round prostrating themselves on their faces, he came in a small double Canoe with few attendants but he was received by the Indians in general with more Ceremony & respect than they paid to the Queen; . . . He is a remarkable fine young fellow of two or three & twenty years of age, strong & well made with a noble Countenance, he bears the Signs of a hard drinker of Ava, he was dressed in an elegant red, black & yellow feathered Cloak with a white Maro or belt, . . . .
>
> —Journals of Captain James Cook, Beaglehole, p. 1227—Samwell

Kaneoneo's appearance on the *Discovery* that day had the touch of melodrama or abject wilfullness, and provided an interesting insight into the matter of rank of which the feathers are such important symbols. Though he was of *pi'o* rank and was granted the *kapu moe*, the prostrating *kapu*, his estranged wife, Kamakahelei, was the hereditary high chiefess and ruler of her islands, Kaua'i and Ni'ihau. And though birth denied her the sacred *kapu moe*, the *kapu* of *pi'o* chiefs, it had granted her everything else and she asserted this aspect of her prerogatives by paying a visit to the strange foreign ships that had sailed into Hawaiian waters. Not to be outdone, Kaneoneo followed suit, racing through the waters of Waimea Bay on Kaua'i in his double canoe. He plowed through the small canoes of commoners as though they were unimportant bits of flotsam in order to reach the *Discovery* before the other royal party had left. The Queen and her party were housed comfortably in the Captain's cabin below decks when Kaneoneo's approach was noted. Kaneoneo's supporters surrounded him protectively for the short time he remained on board on the main deck and refused to agree to his joining the other royal party. Captain Clerke was unaware that the two royal parties thus remained apart.

From the time of this first encounter, the great English explorer and his men were dazzled every day by the continued sight of the chiefs walking about on shore or coming aboard, splendidly clothed in their feather capes or cloaks and helmets.

[1] *This was the first and only appearance of one of the large feather kāhili of Hawai'i during this visit. Many smaller kāhili—often called flyflaps were displayed during the weeks at Kealakekua.*

[2] *Kamakahelei was a hereditary queen of Ni'ihau and Kaua'i. Married now to Ka'eo of the ruling family—the Pi'ilani—of Maui, she had been previously married to Kaneoneo, the pi'o heir to the throne of 'O'ahu. This marriage, it was said, was entered into for dynastic reasons; her present tie to Ka'eo Pi'ilani was a love match. The union to Kaneoneo did not produce heirs.*

[3] *Too-mahana was actually Kaneoneo the son of Kūmahana, a pi'o chief of the highest rank who was the son of Peleioholani of 'O'ahu the last great chief of the KāKuhihewa dynasty of that island. Kūmahana, as well as his son, Kaneoneo, were the offspring of brother and sister unions producing children of the highest rank.*

★*Tamataherei— Kamakahelei*
★*Ta-eoh— Ka'eo*

This young tattooed chief wearing the full regalia of his rank is a stunning representation of feather garments being worn. The sketch was done by Jacques Arago, who came to Hawai'i as a member of the de Freycinét expedition in 1817.
—Courtesy of the Bernice Pauahi Bishop Museum

Captain Cook wrote during his visit to Kaua'i:

They have also neat Tippets made of red and yellow feathers and Caps and Cloaks covered with the same or some other feathers; the cloaks, reach to about the middle of the back, and are like riding cloaks worn in Spain. The Caps are made so as to fit very close to the head with a semicircular protuberance on the crown exactly like the helmets of old.

—Journals of Captain James Cook, Beaglehole, p. 280—Cook

And while on Hawai'i, Captain Clerke made these observations:

They have Cloaks and Caps of Feathers of various kind; the Cloaks about the size, or somewhat smaller than our Ladies short Cloaks or Capuchins; the Caps are more like our light Horsemens Caps than any thing I remember to have seen among us; the groundwork of the Cloak is Net-work, to which the Feathers are made to adhere by Threads with great art and nicety; the most striking of them, I think, are those composed of the red & yellow feathers; these, at a little distance, very strongly resemble a red cloath Cloak, richly ornamented with broad gold Lace; their other cloaks are of various Colours, just as fancy at the time directs. The Ground-work of the Cap is Basket Work, made in a form to fit the Head, to which the Feathers are secured in the same manner as to the Net of the cloaks: these Caps & Cloaks are quite a new manufacture to us, have a beautiful & pleasing Appearance, and I think are altogether very ingenious and pretty.

—Journals of Captain James Cook, Beaglehole, p. 1320—Clerke

One unforgettable day, the Englishmen watched Kalani-'ōpu'u, King of the island of Hawai'i, sail out to the British ships in Kealakekua Bay during the state visit to Captain Cook. He arrived in a flotilla of three double canoes, the second of which carried his priests and feather gods, the *akua hulu manu,* to the visiting British ships. The feather images were laid flat in the middle of a central platform which ran between the stern end of two canoes.

The great gods, personified in wicker (sennit) forms covered with red, black, white and yellow feathers, were a new sight, awesome and fierce but compelling in their overall artistic impact. The high craftsmanship apparent in their making was admired and the artistic achievement seen in each piece was to intrigue the English explorers and their countrymen at home for many years to come.

At Noon Terreeoboo in a large Canoe attended by two others set out from the

Village & paddled towards the Ships in great state. In the first Canoe was Ter-reeoboo, In the Second Kao with 4 Images, the third was fill'd with hogs & Vegetables, as they went along those in the Center Canoe kept Singing with much Solemnity; from which we concluded that this procession had some of their religious ceremoneys mixt with it; but instead of going on board they came to our side, their appearance was very grand, the Chiefs standing up drest in their Cloaks & Caps, & in the Center Canoe were the busts of what we supposd their Gods made of basket work, variously coverd with red, black, white, & Yellow feathers, . . . we drew out our little guard to receive him, & the Capt[n] observing that the King went on shore, followd him. After we had got into the Markee, the King got up & threw in a graceful manner over the Captns Shoulders the Cloak he himself wore, & put a feathered Cap upon his head, & a very handsome fly flap in his hand: Besides which he laid down at the Captains feet 5 or 6 Cloaks more, all very beautiful, & to them of the greatest Value, . . . .

I was surprised to see in the person of this King whose presents & whose train was really Royal, the same old immaciated infirm man that came off to us when were off the NE end of Mowee; & His chief attendants those who staid with us all Night. Amongst these was Maiha-Maiha,[1] whose hair was now Paisted over with a brown dirty sort of Paste or Powder, & which added to as savage a looking face as I ever saw, it however by no means seemed an emblem of his disposition which was good naturd & humorous; Although his manners shew'd shomewhat of an overbearing spirit & he seem'd to be the Principal director in this interview; there were two very handsome Youths[2], the youngest Sons of the King, the oldest of these about 16 years of Age was also on board that night. All which shews the entire confidence they placed in us.

—Journals of Captain James Cook, Beaglehole, p. 512—King

Captain James Cook and members of his company were not only continually impressed by the beauty of Hawaiian feather objects, judging from the frequency of observations in their journals, but also were in a state of wonderment because all of it was so strangely new and unexpected. The texture of the garments, a spin-off of the daring use to which the feathers of extraordinary beauty were put, the complexity of design, and the dramatic absence of information regarding these garments, fanned the fires of mystery and awe surrounding them. Indeed, we are still, two hundred years later, not much further advanced in our knowledge and understanding of Hawaiian featherwork than the people of late 18th Century Europe.

[2] *The two "very handsome youths" were the youngest sons of Kalani-'ōpu'u and his last wife, Kāneka-polei. They were half-brothers of Kalani-'ōpu'u's high born heir, Kiwala'ō.*

[3] *Keoua Kū'ahu'ula and Keoua Pe'eale were sixteen and fourteen years old respectively. Keoua Kū'ahu'ula came later to be involved in fierce and destructive wars against Kamehameha over rulership of the island of Hawai'i. Keoua Pe'eale disappeared from history soon after the arrival of Captain Cook. Keoua Kū'ahu'ula lived on until 1790 when he was killed at Kawaihae during the dedication ceremonies connected with Kamehameha's restoration of the heiau of Pu'u Koholā.*

John Webber, the artist of the third voyage of Captain Cook, made this magnificent sketch in which one of the great royal cloaks is spread across the front of the first canoe where King Kalani-ʻōpuʻu, Kamehameha, and the king's two youngest sons sit while making the official visit to the HMS Resolution. On this occasion, Kalani-ʻōpuʻu set five capes at the feet of Captain Cook and then later took the one he was wearing and draped it over Cook's shoulders. —Courtesy of the Bernice Pauahi Bishop Museum

# The Birds

HE FOUNDATION OF ALL HAWAIIAN FEATHERWORK lies, of course, with certain endemic birds of the Hawaiian forests and surrounding seas who produced feathers of spectacular beauty. The feathers found in *lei* and in the *'ahu'ula,* worked into the basketry frames of helmets and the *akua hulu manu,* and displayed in the *kāhili,* were all taken from birds found in the mountains and along the sharp cliffs or beaches of all the islands. These birds were primarily natives of the islands, highly specialized in eating habits and the products of a uniquely organized and fragile ecosystem of plant and animal life which had evolved during centuries of isolation. They had developed into new forms from an assortment of ancestors. The result was the coming into existence of a biota peculiar to Hawai'i, a spate of birds and plants and insects that were splendidly original. The lobeliads from whose blooms the many species of honeycreeper took nectar, the tree fern or cibotium, the broad leafed *'ape'ape,* the giant *koa* high on the slopes of volcanic mountains and the many varieties of *'ohi'a lehua* all provided food and nesting places. Trees and shrubs thrived in the lush Hawaiian rain forests, where the colorful birds lived, feeding on flower seeds and fruits and the myriad small insects and snails which also inhabited the forests. In many cases, these tiny creatures were as specialized to living in the unique Hawaiian environment as were the plants and birds.

"The Woods are filled with birds of a most beautiful Plumage & some of a very sweet note," wrote the ship's surgeon, Samwell. "We bought many of them alive of the Indians who were employed in catching them with birdlime smeared on the end of a long rod which they thrust between the branches of the trees . . .”

—Journals of Captain James Cook, Beaglehole, p. 1167—Samwell

Another Cook Voyager, Captain Clerke, observed:

> The birds of these Islands are as beautiful as any we have seen during the Voyage; and are numerous though not various. There are four which seem to belong to the Trochili or Honey-Suckers of Linnaeus, one of which is something larger than a Bullfinch; its colour is a fine glossy black, the rump, vent, and thighs deep yellow: another is of an exceeding bright Scarlet colour, the wings and tail black: a third which seems to be either a young bird or variety of the Foregoing is variegated with red, brown and yellow; the fourth is entirely green with a tinge of yellow.

—Journals of Captain James Cook, Beaglehole, p. 602—Clerke

Among the birds Captain Clerke described were the *mamo* which produced darkish yellow feathers, and the *'i'iwi* which provided the main source of red feathers. He has also described the *'apapane,* the green *'ō'ū* and finally the *'ō'ō* with its long *'ē'ē* feathers of pale yellow. These were the first particular birds from which feathers were taken to fashion the gods, the helmets, cloaks and *lei.*

“There is also,” Clerke wrote, “a bird with a long tail whose colour is black, the vent, and feathers under the wings (which are much longer than is usually seen in the generality of birds except the birds of Paradise), are yellow . . .”

*The magnificent Frigate Bird, or kalae'iwa, which lives high in the cliffs of Hawai'i's mountain ranges or at the seashore among naupaka and pōhue vines. Kalae'iwa provide a greenish black feather which grew between its wings. It is a bird of great strength and endurance, much admired by Hawaiians of olden times.*

# 'Akialoa

*Hemignathus obscurus*

This seven inch long honeycreeper and its subspecies once graced 'O'ahu, Lana'i and Hawai'i. The bird and a related species on Kaua'i *(Hemignathus procerus)* are now presumed extinct. During its prime in the 1800s, the *'akialoa* ate insects, but was known as a nectar lover, using its long beak and tongue to extract honey from *lehua* and the *hāhā* and *'ōhā-wai,* both native lobelia. The birds were sighted in *mauka* and *makai* forests, often in large *koa* trees. Here they stayed, singing freely—a brief, energetic trill, especially vigorous and carefree.

# 'I'iwi

*Vestiaria coccinea*

The *'i'iwi* is fairly common in the upper forests of Hawai'i, Maui and Kaua'i, but is almost extinct on 'O'ahu and Moloka'i. The five and a half inch long bird flies farther than most honeycreepers in search of *'ōhi'a* and lobelia blossoms, and its strong wings can be heard flapping far away. When a lobelia is found, the *'i'iwi* swings upside down, sticks its head and bill into the flower and feeds. A few seconds later, onto the next *pua*. Its song has been called "harsh, strained and discordant," which helps it defend a larger territory than many native birds.

# ‘Ō‘ū

*Psittirostra psittacea*

The *‘ō‘ū* once inhabited all the Islands, but this seven inch long bird is now the rarest honeycreeper, found only on the Big Island's windward coast and in Kaua‘i's Alaka‘i Swamp. The *‘ō‘ū* is known for its lengthy, high altitude flights, which take the birds to new feeding grounds. Once there, its parrot-like bill is ideal for eating berries, fruits, blossoms and leaves. The *‘ō‘ū* has a sweet, beautiful voice, which it enjoys sharing in the early morning when perched on the highest branch. Though never seen, its nests probably hide among the staghorn fern and *‘ie‘ie* vine.

# 'Apapane

*Himatione Sanguinea*

The *'apapane* is found throughout Hawai'i's *koa* and *'ōhi'a* forests, where it flits from *lehua* to *lehua,* stopping to sip the nectar for a few seconds before moving onto another blossom or insect. Averaging five and a quarter inches long, the numerous honeycreepers (also known as the *'akahane*) have strong wings which can be heard buzzing in the wind as they fly across the islands. The birds have so many different calls and songs that one ornithologist called their musicianship "unsurpassed." The high-rising *'ōhi'a* is home for the *'apapane.*

# Hawai'i 'Ō'ō

*Moho nobilis*

Kaua'i, 'O'ahu, Moloka'i and Hawai'i each had its own species of 'ō'ō, but the Big Island's was the largest—about 12 inches—and the one most sought after by the *ali'i's* bird catchers. The 'ō'ō's popularity and shrinking forests resulted in extinguishing all but a dozen birds that may remain on Kaua'i. When alive, some ornithologists said the Hawai'i 'ō'ō was timid and wary, hiding in the tallest trees, where it fed on nectar and insects. Others called it aggressive. Most agreed it had a distinct song that was beautiful and haunting, but rarely heard.

# Mamo

*Drepanis pacifica*

Not much is known about this eight inch long honeycreeper, which has not been seen on the Big Island, its only home, since 1898. Even before this, the bird was probably uncommon and its feathers were the most highly prized. It once flew all over the island's forests (feeding primarily on the nectar of lobelia), where native Hawaiians hid to capture the *mamo* for their *ali'i*. Some said the bird was easily managed; others called it wild and shy. Whatever its temperament, the natives imitated the bird's cry—a long, solitary and sorrowful note—and the *mamo* generally responded and was ensnared.

*Kau-i-ke-aoŭli, the youngest son of Kamehameha and Keʻōpuolani (he later became Kamehameha III), wearing a cloak and carrying a kāhili lele. (Opposite page) His sister, Harieta Nāhiʻenaʻena, wearing a cape over her shoulders and feathers in her hair. She too carries a kāhili lele. At one time, this full brother and sister lived together, hoping to produce a royal heir of the piʻo rank. —Etchings by William Dampier, courtesy of the Honolulu Academy of Arts*

# Cultural Manifestations

OTHING HAS COME DOWN—in writing or from oral sources—to tell us why certain designs were used in capes, cloaks and *lei*. Why the color schemes in these patterns? Why the particular choice of feathers? Yet, these features reach out from the objects themselves, demanding recognition of philosophic or artistic merit and declaring the powerful manifestation of a culture and of its genius.

A great deal of featherwork was collected during Captain Cook's visits of 1778 and 1779. The chiefs, in a frenzy of admiration, brought treasured helmets, capes and cloaks to the ships. Some brought feather objects to use in bartering forays. Kamehameha himself sold an "elegant feathered Cloak, which he brought to sell but would part with it for nothing but iron Daggers". (Journals of Captain James Cook, Beaglehole, p. 1190—Samwell). He took nine daggers in exchange for the cloak.

Members of Captain Cook's company all reacted with a surprising degree of interest and amazement, which is the way the feathers struck me when I first saw them as a child. Their description, however, varied: Samwell was more intrigued with the colors in the feather garments than the details of their making; Cook, on the other hand, emphasized these attributes. Lieutenant King was greatly impressed with the number of feathers that went into the making of a cloak, cape or feather god. Samwell seemed particularly captivated by the sight of birds, their plumage, their numbers and their songs.

In all the writings of the men of Captain James Cook's exploring expeditions, not one—not one—has written anything about the meaning of the designs or color schemes found in Hawai'i featherwork. This creates the need we have today to probe into possible meanings, despite the great void of information.

What intrigued me most of all about featherworks, from the earliest time on, were the designs one found. Why the lines? Why the triangles? Why the curves? Why the reds? Why the blacks and, in rare cases, greens? Why the yellow background? Some garments were far more suggestive of mystical affinities than others. Some chiefs designed garments of abstract design suggesting time and space. Cosmic, powerful lines flow across these garments. Distortions of triangular shapes and lines shoot like rays of light from the yellow or red. Other designs were more of this earth, using simple everyday forms.

There's one garment which previously was in the Lever collection in London's Lever Museum, and which is now in Vienna at the Volkerkunde Museum. It is astounding. To me it has very strange lines; they look almost animal-like. It looks like a great bird in flight—in slow flight. My feeling about it is—immediately!—'aumakua. Perhaps the chief who wore it had a connection to the owl. The designs appear to be more than just lines set down at whim, their placement more than just haphazard. They are certainly not happenstance arrangements, but carefully considered elements of form worked into patterns which are mainly concerned with an exhibition of symbols relating to clan, to the spiritual connections with 'aumakua. (guardian spirits), and the constant tie existing between the wearer of feather garments and the universe.

*The great Queen Ka'ahumanu, wearing a tiny lei in the unique style she preferred. —Sketch by Louis Choris, courtesy of the Honolulu Academy of Arts.*

[1]*Mana —the source of spiritual power, the source of intelligence and excellence. Mana was hidden in the divine ancestry of a person. Mana was hidden in the kaona (the metaphor) of chants. Mana —elusive and subtle, much sought after but not easily attained, —therefore you put the best of your heart and soul, your feelings and hopes, into a work of art! The designs on feather objects and garments were particularly challenging to the old Hawaiian artists. In their mana-steeped consciousness these artists worked always to achieve the most generous acquisition of mana. Mana was granted or collected in objects to the degree the maker put heart and soul into the creation. Inspiration came from the gods. One kept in constant touch with unseen powers. Prayers and chants and certain rituals fortified this union between artist and akua.*

There is much that is heavenly, or celestial if you will in Hawaiian feather garments, ornaments and religious objects. They seem to say that there is more than just the decorative in their appearance. They represent, in design, definitive statements of kinship connections to family gods—the 'aumakua—and to the kū'auhau—the family genealogies.

One of my feelings is that if you should see a particular chief in a cloak, on whatever occasion, you would know from his 'ahu'ula that he was wearing something of his clan, something related to the 'aumakua he worshipped—and you would certainly see in his feathers expressions of his personal or family ties to the cosmic.

The designs could be the coat-of-arms of the wearer. They could be symbolic because they represent, in some mysterious way, a relationship of one individual to a larger group. There is an element of heraldry here, a notice of authority and rank. There is also a strong mystical element that recalls the spiritual leanings of its designer. The marks found on objects of old Hawai'i were placed there to make a point, a point exceeding the purely decorative. The opportunity to use symbols to dramatize artistic or intellectual possibilities was never overlooked. You also see this in petroglyphs and kapa designs and in the Hawaiian quilting traditions of the last and present century.

What do we see in these artistic statements? Circles?—a few. Triangles?—also a few. Fin-like shapes? 'Aumakua?—probably. So close was the connection of everyday man and his daily routine to the kūpuna, the gods and the 'aumakua that recognition of them is strong in all Hawaiian art. The capes and cloaks were an excellent place to implant lines and forms which gave emphasis to these connections. So strong is the link between the symbolic and the real that the actual subsides in importance. It is too ordinary. Too mundane and lacking in mana[1]. There is in ancient Hawai'i a constant push toward the unreal, toward the unordinary. Myths and legends abound. The skies are searched for "signs". Signs give direction. Signs are far-fetched, comfortably removed from terra firma. The imagination is alive with possibilities, flashed into consciousness by stimuli removed from objective restrictions. Dim forms in clouds, patterns of motion in trees and shrubs, the ocean currents, the motion of breaking waves, the color of the sea—all nature gave direction to the cogitations of an old time Hawaiian. The rhythms found in growth, the vibrations of earth and sky, the life of the sea, the feel of the wind, the fall of the rain, the flights and calls of birds—the shriek of the 'io, or the boatswain bird's call, the cry of the red pouched kalae'iwa, the calls of the treasured woodland birds with their crops of gold, black, red and green feathers—all exuded nature signals. Nature spoke out and man heeded.

There is evidence of the gods in Pele and Kama-pua'a in Hi'iaka and Lohi'au. Kāne, Kū, Lono and Kanaloa are everywhere. They have endless variation—Kāne of the thunder cloud, Kāne of the woodlands, Kāne of the sparkling waters, Kū of the mountain tops, Kū of the koa trees, Kū of the cloudy heavens and so forth. The same was true of 'Io and hosts of lesser gods. Malo and Emerson have recorded hundreds of ritual prayers. In reading these prayers we can understand how important it was for the Hawaiians of the older days to link themselves to the unseen, the universal realm of the gods. In the motions of the *hula* one sees the imagination of old Hawai'i reaching to the skies, to the mountains and trees, to the universe.

Animals given the *'aumakua* significance possessed powers beyond those with which they are naturally endowed. Sharks were an important *'aumakua* to all classes of people in old Hawai'i. They are creatures of great strength and ferocity. This may be why the *niho-mano,* shark teeth, are so widely used in the design of feather garments. To this very day Hawaiian families lay serious claim to the *'aumakua* relationship of the shark. They offer protection that is both supernatural and ordinary, as of the earth.

A chief wrapped in a cloak which has been imbued with such powers could feel that divinely given *mana* would not be invaded or harmed during times of high political ceremony, battles or religious rituals, times when he would likely wear these creations.

Did the chiefs, in wearing the feather garments, actually become birds wearing "borrowed" or "given" feathers? They had god-like status by virtue of birth, so what are the sexual implications in wearing feather garments? They easily could have assumed the role of giant male birds of brilliant plumage wrapped in the clever and stunning fabrications devised by humans. Birth, family and guardian angel implanted in a surface of fiber, woven with great skill and artistic genius give the feather garments of old Hawai'i a *supra* human quality. Examined closely or looked at from a short distance they sometimes appear to be too sacred, too strange, too artistic for mundane human use, as though the exalted places they have in the world's museums is their truest and noblest destiny. They are sacred relics, to be seen and admired or even loved, from a distance.

We are often surprised to learn that birds of such surpassing beauty as the quetzelcoatl of Mexico, the gorgeous bird of paradise of New Guinea, or the lyre bird of Australia are domestic per se. Despite their extraordinary appearances, they fulfill the routine duties of all birds. They gather food, nest and carefully tend to their young.

Equally surprising, and enough to arouse our curiosity, were the chiefs. They were like birds of brilliant plumage in their social role, which was partly pomp and show. They were into looking good, or, more than that, looking colorful and above the every day commonness of the work-a-day world. By virtue of their *mana* or spiritual rank they demonstrated their separateness, or certainly their being different. At the same time they were able to manage the daily routines of the community with cool, calm expertise.

The brilliance of their color, and the mystery of the designs worked into each garment, are as representational as anything can be in art. And the gods are linked by color, design and substance to the chiefs and high chiefs who wore these garments.

In some respects, the feather garments have a dull, repetitive look. The half crescents and fins are used repeatedly in the design of both cloaks and capes, and yet, they are not tiresome because they are used differently in each garment. Longer crescents, half crescents, longer fins, fatter fins, more red than yellow, more black than usual. I sometimes feel that there is a static in these works because they are so different from anything else that we encounter in a peoples' art—they're so *different*. We know the value of the feathers. We know the enormous amount of work it took to collect them, we know how few yellow feathers there were to collect and how many went into the making of even a small cape. We know all of these wonderful things. Sometimes the end results seem to be heavy and rather lifeless in relation to western art. My thinking has been shaped primarily by looking at western art and judging other art with the principles embodied in western paintings and sculpture. A narrow view. A view prejudiced by my thinking, by the influences on me. I am greatly affected by Renaissance art or western art, and particularly by Renaissance art where there is so much activity, color, a high priority placed on representational factors. Look at a Greek vase. You can say that it's monotonous because there are so very few lines and a monochromatic color scheme, black and brown with a little bit of tan. There are figures, some of them doing quite naughty things on those vases, or Greek containers, but though they might hold your interest for a moment, they can also seem quite dull. Even a great Renaissance painting, I suppose, if you looked at it long enough, would appear sooner or later to be dull in some ways.

I am half-Hawaiian, but at times I can look at a piece of featherwork made by some of my ancestors (and probably worn by some of them) and be quite disinterested. And yet, when you get away from some mundane details: How many feathers? How many hours or years did it take to make one of these garments? Tales about the poor suffering birds. When you see them one after the other, time after time, not behind glass but in all their naturalness and variety (no two are exactly alike), you are struck again and again with their force and the ingenuity of their creation and you marvel once again that these are only a part of the magnificent heritage of Old Hawai'i.

Consider *kapa* (and its hundreds of designs and colors so different from those found in capes and cloaks), wood sculpture figures, and canoes and calabashes, and one marvels at the creative productivity of Hawaiians. At some future time, I would like to examine the artistic achievement of Hawaiian wood carving and go from there to look at what can be seen as manifestations of grace and excellence in the work-a-day tools and objects created by this old culture.

# *Lei Hulu*

*A LEI HULU* OF HAWAI'I were designed and made to be used by women. These feather creations were worn twisted in hair atop women's heads (as shown in the famous sketch by John Webber), and they were worn in a stunning fashion around the neck as well. The designing of patterns for *lei* seemed to be aimed at producing a light, decorative effect. Texture also played a role in the final appearance of *lei hulu.* The fine orange, yellow patterns of *mamo,* called *ko'o mamo,* and the paler yellow *'ē'ē* feathers of the *'ō'ō,* gave the strongest aspect of texture to *lei.* Some yellow *lei* have a downy lightness, as though made from goose down. Others look more compact, more distinctly cylindrical. These *lei* made of yellow feathers alone were also the most valued *lei,* due perhaps to their scarcity. *'Ō'ō* and *mamo* both produced limited numbers of feathers useful to the Hawaiian featherwork artist. Other *lei* were patterned of black, red and green feathers. Attractive arrangements or groupings of different colors in *lei* called *paukū* resulted in ornamental creations of rare beauty. Some *lei* were given a spiral effect, as for example the green used in the yellow and red *lei* of the Holt collection. These are called *lei pani'o.* Another style of *lei* is one called *kāmoe.* It has an entirely different character, with its feathers laid down on the backing.

> In the voyages of Captains Portlock and Dixon in 1786 we read: "But the most beautiful ornament worn by the women is a necklace made from the variegated feathers of the humming bird which are fixed on strings so regular and even as to have a surface equally smooth as velvet; and the rich colours of the feathers give it an appearance equally rich and elegant."
>
> —Brigham, Vol. #1 p. 7

My Aunt Ellen used to say to me: "I used to love to go to my grandmother Bubu's house on Punchbowl Street, especially on the days that she was airing her feather *leis* and her feather capes. She had two capes and over fifty *leis.*" Aunt Ellen would say that she would only see her wearing one or, at the most, two *leis* at a time. Sometimes she would let Aunt Lizzie and Aunt Annie—her daughters— wear *leis.* Never did we have the sight of fifty *leis* being out at one time. She would have them all pinned to a valance of her four poster bed to hang so that the air could circulate around them and her Hawaiian house-hold women would run their hands gently down the feathers to put warmth and body oils into the feathers. "Bubu said it kept the feathers *eu-eu,* lively and shining. After this, she would put the *leis* back in her camphor chests. The sight of those *leis* was so beautiful— and those little capes! She would always say, in Hawaiian of course, [because] she didn't speak English, [that] 'someday some of these feathers will go to you, Ellen, and you must learn to take care of them and you must treat them with great respect: You must love them with your heart—because they are your *'ohana,* they are your relatives.' I would then think to myself, going home to Fort Street in her Barouche, 'What in God's name did she mean

Queen Ka'ahumanu wearing a simple red, 'i'iwi lei. —Painting by Louis Choris, courtesy of the Honolulu Academy of Arts

(Preceding pages) Leis painted in water color by Sarah Stone, which were in a collection at the Lever Museum in London before it was disbanded. —Courtesy of the Bernice Pauahi Bishop Museum

that they were my relatives?'" Aunt Ellen would ask around among her older relatives. One uncle would talk and another one wouldn't. "I'd ask oldtimers—old family friends or the great uncles or Tutu Mauloa—and they would say, 'Of course, the *leis* are part of your family. The *leis* are like children. Bubu is saying that you have to treat them like members of your family because they are so precious. They were made very carefully, very lovingly and they were highly treasured.'"

But you wouldn't think they were such objects of love at the rate they were being swished around when Captain Cook came and, when other traders came through, you would have thought they were just cheaper by the dozen. The time my Aunt Ellen was speaking of—around the 1890s, when my great grandmother lived on Punchbowl Street below Kawaiahao Church—in that day and age they were highly regarded and very highly treasured. I know from other stories aside from my Aunt Ellen's about Hanakaulani's feathers. A young man who used to be one of the queen's—Queen Lili'uokalani's—coachman, probably a footman who drove some of the time to relieve the coachman, told me about his experiences at Apua, my great grandmother's home. His name was Joe Nicholas and he lived down in Waikiki on a little plot of land that the queen had given his family. He told me several times about going down to Punchbowl Street to pick up Hanakaulani. He said, "Oh, I used to love to go—the queen would send me down to pick her up. I used to love to go on the days that she had her *leis* out because, remember now, I was just a coachman and I had to be very careful. I'd go up the stairs and call for her. That tall, tall Chinese butler that they had, Jackson was his name, would sort of keep me standing there. Hanakaulani would be in another part of the house. I'd go and peek in her bedroom window, the front bedroom right on the veranda. These long windows ran down to the floor and I would peek in to see if the feathers were out and, if the feathers were out, it was such a sight to see all of these leis—so many of them."

These stories made me feel good. They were a verification of very private, inside-of-the-family information. I definitely had the experience of being taught as a young person how valuable these things were to the Hawaiians and how much they meant to us, how much they had to be cared for, loved. People who made them, who wore them, who had strong feelings as my grandmother did, thought in terms of giving them love. When she aired them she would run her hands down the length of a *lei*. She would say things in Hawaiian to them as if she were talking to children. Among some of us Hawaiians there is high regard for these old works. Designs and color formations so lively in every one that you see. Even in the pure yellow, in the 'ō'ō and the *mamo lei*, there is something exquisitely beautiful that never suggests a deadness or a dullness and I get the feeling that the *lei* had this feeling. To me they always were strangely beautiful things, never dull, never static, never the sort of art that was contrived or strained too hard to express itself as art. It came out of a strong spiritual foundation.

There is an odd mixture of Oxford and Hawai'i in this photo of Lawrence Kentwell, shown in graduation robes after completing studies at New College, Oxford. He was the husband of Anne Holt. He is wearing four mamo lei hulu tied together. They belonged to my great grandmother Hana-kaulani-o-Kamāmalu. —Photo courtesy of Mr. & Mrs. John Dominis Holt IV

The well known Elizabeth K. Booth was descended from Mrs. John Baker, the high chiefess Noa-Noa, from whom she inherited her splendid feather objects and her lands. Among her holdings were what is now Saint Louis Heights, Pacific Heights and the neighborhood known as Pauoa.

(Opposite page) The high chiefess, Mele Kaupoko, wearing a lei of ko-o mamo feathers.

My great grandmother Hana-kaulani-o-Kamāmalu, daughter of Ka-malo-o-Leleihoku and Lord George Paulet. She was the wife of Owens Jones Holt, and the mistress of his ranches at Halemano, Waialua and Mākaha.

(Opposite page) This was one of the last photographs of Princess Ka'iulani. Shortly after it was made, she went to the island of Hawai'i to visit the Parkers. During one of her favorite pastimes—riding horseback—she was caught in a heavy downpour at the edges of Ke'eaumoku Forest. She contracted pneumonia and was returned to Honolulu in a stretcher. Two weeks later, she was dead at age 23.

*These leis from the Bernice Pauahi Bishop Museum Collection are made in both the paukū and pāniʻo style.—Photo by Seth Joel, courtesy of the Bernice Pauahi Bishop Museum*

*(Opposite page) This collection of leis is from my great-grandmother, Hanakaulani-o-Kamāmalu. The feathers are from the ʻōʻō, mamo and ʻōʻū birds.*

This unusual green and red lei was worn on the head. It was acquired by the Honolulu Academy of Arts in 1927. The yellow, black and red spiral lei is a good example of this style of lei hulu. It was acquired by Mrs. C. M. Cooke for the Honolulu Academy of Arts from a part-Hawaiian family for $350.00 in 1929. —Photo by Bob Chinn, courtesy of the Honolulu Academy of Arts

(Opposite page) A magnificent example of the pāni'o technique of lei making of old Hawai'i. —Photo by Ben Patnoi, courtesy of the Bernice Pauahi Bishop Museum

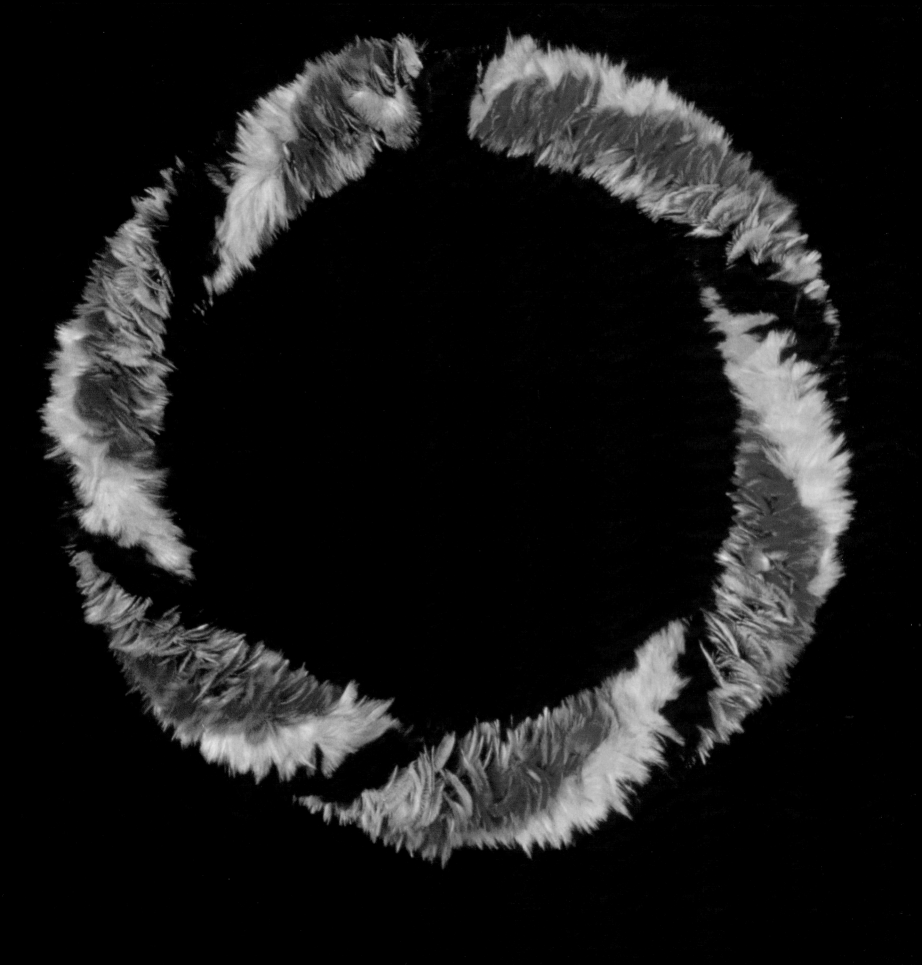

This lei mamo (top) belonged to the high chiefess Kalakua, the grandmother of King Lunalilo. It was presented to R. C. L. Perkins by someone whose mother had been given the lei by Charles Kanaina, the father of King Lunalilo. Mr. Perkins, who was sent to Hawai'i to collect birds and bird lore by Lord Walter Rothschild, took the lei to England in 1892. It was returned and given anonymously to the Honolulu Academy of Arts in 1951. The larger 'ō'ō, 'ē'ē lei is an excellent example of the larger of the two kinds of yellow leis. It was a gift from W. Damon Giffard to the Honolulu Academy of Arts. The lei belonged to his grandmother Mattie Brickwood Giffard. —Courtesy of the Honolulu Academy of Arts

(Opposite page) A paukū lei made in the unique kāmoe style. —Photo by Ben Patnoi, courtesy of the Bernice Pauahi Bishop Museum

These striking lei hulu show a different technique in making the 'ō'ū and mamo-'ō'ō paukū leis. The feathers are looser than those seen in the kāmoe style, which presses the feathers to their full length against the center, the central kumu foundation of the lei. The mamo, 'ō'ō, 'i'iwi, 'ō'ū and the black 'ō'ō centerpiece of this lei hulu are in excellent condition. Mixed colored leis such as these were not worn for regal occasions. At such times, mamo and then 'ō'ō leis of pure yellow were preferred. These lei hulu were a gift to the Honolulu Academy of Arts from Wilhelmina Tenney, daughter of Rose Makee Tenney, one of the famous Makee sisters of Ulupalakua Ranch. —Courtesy of the Honolulu Academy of Arts

(Opposite page) A lei made from the feathers of the shorter mamo and the longer 'ē'ē feathers of the 'ō'ō.—Photo by Ben Patnoi, courtesy of the Bernice Pauahi Bishop Museum

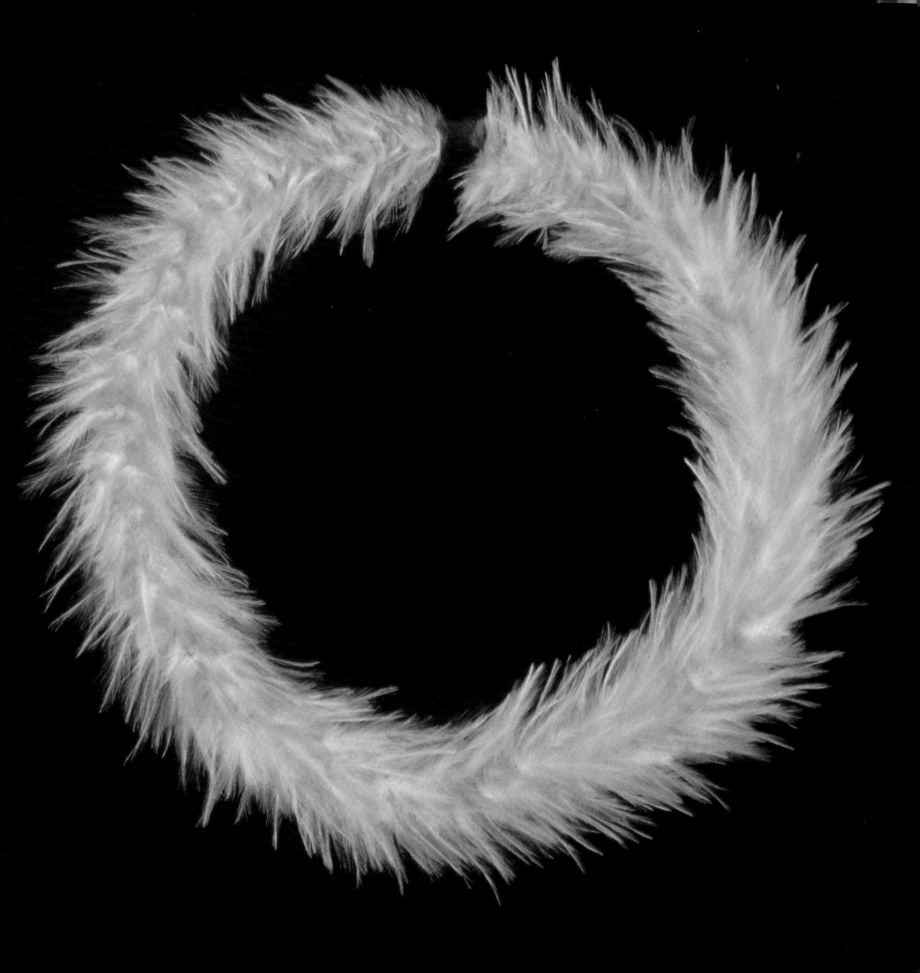

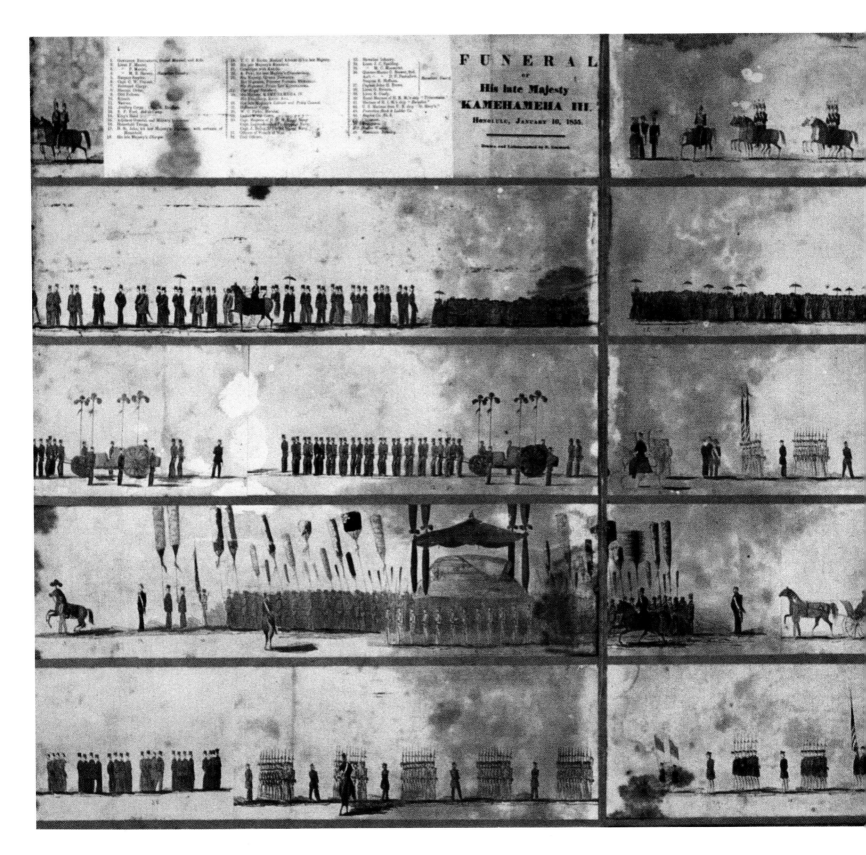

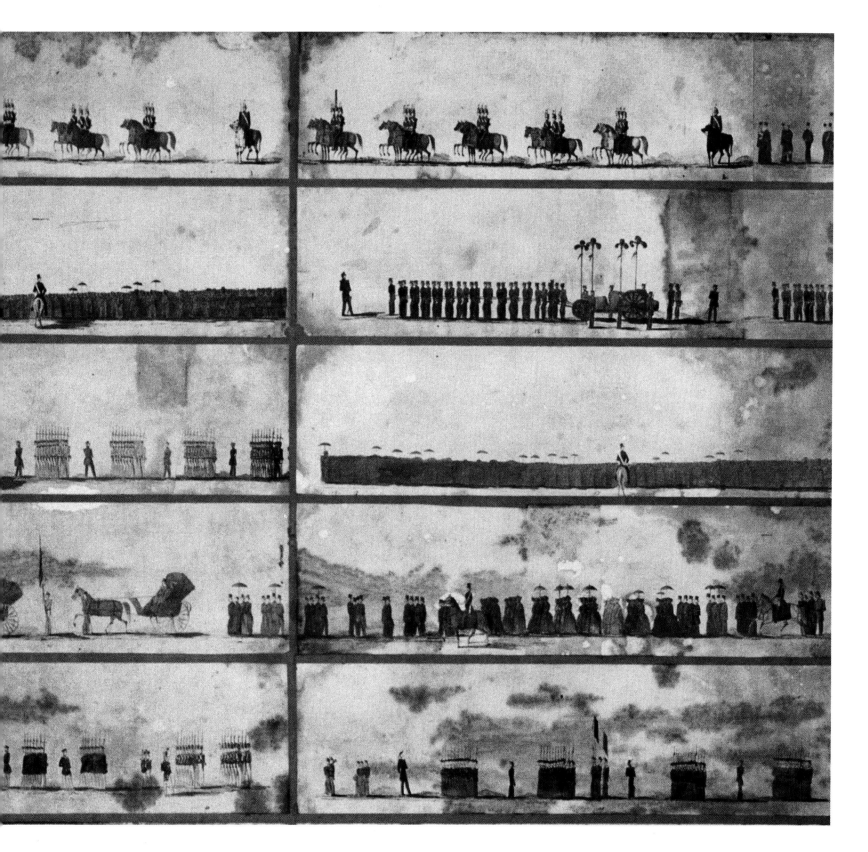

# Kāhili

HE *KĀHILI,* LARGE OR SMALL, were carried by men and boys. The large *kāhili* were emblems of state consisting of a tall pole atop which a cylindrically shaped plume was covered with tufts of bird feathers.

The *kāhili* were made from a variety of feathers—from tail and breast feathers of jungle fowl or from the *kalaeʻiwa,* the frigate bird. Sometimes feathers of the boatswain bird were used, especially the tail feathers which created a powerful effect when massed atop a tall pole. *Kāhili* were buried in *kaona,* in mystery and hidden meaning.

In both the *akua hulu manu* and the *kāhili,* which have always struck me with awe and with a certain degree of fear and trembling, the same effect was achieved abstractly in the form of these strange objects, in the color and texture of their feathers, and in the nature of the purposes they served. All the above was achieved with a great simplicity.

The *kāhili* standards of royalty assumed their particular character and form in the way their feathers were put to use and by the nature of the feathers used. They were made mostly from the feathers of sea birds. The use of such feathers helped to create the fearsome character of the *kāhili.*

The feathers of sea birds are harsh and compelling when compared to the softer yellow, green, red and black feathers taken from smaller birds. In close scrutiny one observes that the velvet-like effect created by feathers of forest birds, which Captain Cook and members of his company noted, is totally different from the tough, plain-toned feathers used in creating the *kāhili.*

They are simple in form—a cylinder made of various kinds of feathers sitting atop a long pole 10 to 25 feet tall—and the weird feathers command recognition of ancient *kapu* in much the same way as did the simple sticks bound at their tops with bundles of white *kapa* or bedecked with streamers of the same—the *kapu* sticks of old.

Some *kāhili* are made of the tails of the boatswain bird, the *koʻae* of Old Hawaiʻi. These birds' tails are made up of tough, greyish-red feathers, and they are easily detached from the bird. They were collected in large quantities from Necker and Nihoa Island.

The harshness of sea bird feathers, especially those of the *kalaeʻiwa* frigate bird, add a distinctly forbidding look to such *kāhili.*[1] Strangely curled and metallic in appearance and of an eerie greenish black color, these feathers seem to have been chosen because they add just that degree of awesomeness which gives the *kāhili* their god-like importance.

The *kalaeʻiwa* is a fierce-looking bird. With its great red pouch blown to the size of a small balloon when the bird is aroused, it is a threatening sight. Its beak is a long, hooked affair protruding form a flat roundish head, and its large, beadish eyes—which can spot fish from hundreds of feet in the air—stare out with anger or suspicion. This creature lives on *naupaka* branches and low slung beach heliotrope bushes, where it builds sparse nests of the dried twigs of both these shrubs.

These *kāhili,* which were individually named, served as protective agents and were abstract in form and decorative in appearance. They are described as emblems of royalty in

*John Dominis Holt II on the front lanai of 'Iolani Palace during the funeral ceremony held for King David Kalākaua in January of 1891. —Courtesy of Mr. and Mrs. John Dominis Holt IV*

*(Preceding pages) This Paul Emmert drawing of King Kamehameha III's funeral shows the mass of kāhili which surrounded the catafalque. The long, narrow ones are uncommon, none exist today. —Courtesy of the Hawaii State Archives*

use on state occasions attended by such observers as Lord Byron and William Richards.

Hand *kāhili,* or *kāhili lele,* were carried by chief and held before them at certain times. *Ali'i nui* Kalani-'ōpu'u, for example, was carrying a *kāhili lele* when he paid the official visit to Captain Cook at Kealakekua. *Kāhili lele* were waved over the heads of *ali'i* to ward off bad *mana*—not to chase flies. The famed artist Choris sketched Queen Ka'ahumanu with a *kāhili lele* being waved above her by her famous dwarf *kahu.*

The most impressive use of *kāhili* were in royal funerals of the 19th Century. During the funeral of Kamehameha III in 1854, many *kāhili* of all sizes and colors surrounded the King's catafalque and created a massive statement of native Hawaiian featherwork. The event was described in native Hawaiian language and foreign newspapers alike. Paul Emmert, a recently arrived European artist who was obviously moved by the sight of *kāhili,* made pastel and pencil drawings of the funeral procession on that occasion. The Paul Emmert drawing certainly shows the mass of *kāhili* and the variety of shapes these took. The long narrow ones are uncommon; none exist today. The illustration of *kāhili* used during Queen Emma's funeral is also outstanding. The sloping position they are given over the coffin adds to the dramatic, moribund appearance of the scene. Equally awesome were the *kāhili* used in the funerals of later royalty. There is a somber, silent beauty to these objects and, indeed, *kāhili* are thus probably the most impelling of all the featherwork arts of Old Hawai'i.

(Above, Top) Princess Ruth, pictured here, loved the honor of being able to use kāhili. Her attendants are John Cummins and Samuel Parker, both of whom were the sons of Hawaiian mothers of high rank.—Courtesy of the Hawaii State Archives

(Right) In this sketch of Queen Emma's funeral from the London Illustrated News, one is struck by the unique way the kāhili are slanted, so that the feathers almost cover the coffin.—Courtesy of the Hawaii State Archives

*The blackish-green feathers used in these kāhili are from the frigate or man-o-war bird, the ka-laeʻiwa. —Photo by Ben Patnoi, courtesy of the Bernice Pauahi Bishop Museum*

*These little kāhili are made from chicken feathers awesomely arranged to create a spiralling effect. The handles are made from tortoise shell, whale bone and possibly kauila wood. —Photo by Ben Patnoi, courtesy of the Bernice Pauahi Bishop Museum*

*The brown feathers used in these kāhili are taken from the wings of mynah birds. —Photo by Ben Patnoi, courtesy of the Bernice Pauahi Bishop Museum*

This striking kāhili lele is made from parrot feathers and a few clusters of 'i'iwi and 'ō'ō. At one time there were flocks of wild parrots in and around Honolulu, many of which had gone wild after being introduced as pets. Others were released by visiting sailors, who in their time were great collectors of exotic birds, especially parrots. —Photo by Ben Patnoi, courtesy of the Bernice Pauahi Bishop Museum

*These kāhili are made from the tail and wing feathers of seabirds. The handles are traditional, made from pieces of tortoise shell and whale bone. —Photo by Ben Patnoi, courtesy of the Bernice Pauahi Bishop Museum*

An assortment of white feathers taken from various birds and fowl used by 19th century kāhili makers. The long feathers in the kāhili at the far left are the tail feathers of white leghorn roosters. The smallest kāhili in this group, second from the left, is made from the tail feathers of a seabird. The tall kāhili, third from left, is made from duck feathers. The other two are unknown and are not to be found in records of the Bernice Pauahi Bishop Museum. —Photo by Ben Patnoi, courtesy of the Bernice Pauahi Bishop Museum

# *Akua Hulu Manu*

ITH THE *AKUA HULU MANU* we see god forms given strongly anthropomorphic appearances. They are ferocious looking, and we view them in fear. They demonstrate with force, power and a certain no-nonsense ugliness that godly power is fearsome. The artist of Old Hawaiʻi created his feather-covered gods to look human and yet, at the same time, bestial. Gaping mouths filled with shark or dog teeth, and forbidding orb-like eyes on oddly shaped heads, achieved a look that could only inspire submission if not reverence. I look at their long necks, the angry expressions, the dog teeth, and I am impressed. I am impressed artistically. There is a wonderful distortion in these figures. In their madness they seem to have humor. In the anger and in the seriousness there seems to be a playful mockery which adds yet another dimension to their meaning. There is a connection between what they look like and what their function might have been.

Brigham says "these gods were carried into battle on *kauwila* poles, most of them having no other sufficient support, also being too small to be placed over the head of a priest, as has been suggested" (Brigham, Vol. #1, p. 36).

They certainly were not out to do battle with Captain Cook when Kalani-ʻōpuʻu took the ones that he owned to the *Discovery* and the *Resolution* on a friendly visit of state. The *akua hulu manu* were objects that symbolized power that was greater than man's. Unearthly power—sky power—heaven power—god power—however you wish to express it. They were objects that represented unseen powers at work, powers far removed from man's limited range of activity. If you can develop an argument that Hawaiians were a war-loving people, that they were fighting and performing human sacrifices all of the time, then you don't have to talk about the artistry of their god images, or the artistry of their capes, cloaks and their helmets, or the magnificent *kāhili,* or even the artistry of their culture for that matter, because you have already laid stress on the war and human sacrifice aspects of Hawaiian life. Many foreign observers have found this a sufficient point to dwell upon. It seemed to blind them to examination or consideration of the ethical, religious, artistic and philosophical elements of Hawaiian life which are elaborately present in their featherwork art. Webber painted *akua hulu manu* in three places, always showing them as gods with a variety of functions.

Two of the *akua* surviving through the nineteenth century are in the collection of the Bernice Pauahi Bishop Museum. One is in very poor shape, badly torn on one side and virtually bare of feathers; the other is, fortunately, almost totally covered with its original and beautiful red feathers. This latter one is the least inspiring of the *akua hulu manu* I have seen. It is studiously anthropomorphic, almost a portrait of a particular person, and it is the least fearsome of all existing *akua hulu manu*. It has come to be known as the Kamehameha Kukaʻilimoku because it is said to be the one given by Kalani-ʻōpuʻu to Kamehameha during ceremonies at Pakini Heiau, where the aging chief divided the rule of the Hawaiian kingdom between his *piʻo* rank son, Kiwalaʻo, and his high-born nephew, Paiʻea Kamehameha.

Akua hulu manu painted by Fredda B. Holt.

(Preceding pages, left to right) Akua with stringy human hair. The feathers are mainly from the ʻiʻiwi bird.

This same akua, or one very similar, was sketched by artist John Webber.

The yellow streak in the middle of the head and around the base of this akua figure give it a unique appearance.

This youthful looking akua was perhaps made for young people. —All images from the Stone Collection, photos courtesy of the Bernice Pauahi Bishop Museum

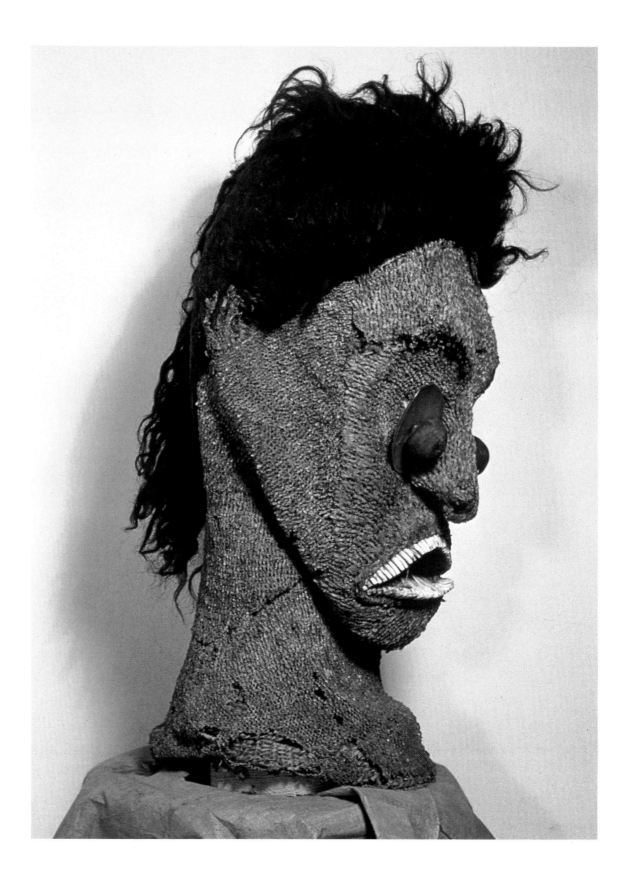

*Badly damaged akua hulu manu. The human hair is intact but the feathers that once covered it are gone. —Courtesy of the Bernice Pauahi Bishop Museum*

*There is an added ferocity to the look of this akua image by virtue of its torn state. The frontal view with the eyes loosened from their sockets and the tear in the area of the ear, which appears to be a great wound, give the image a look of madness or severe injury. —Courtesy of the Bernice Pauahi Bishop Museum*

This god seems to have been designed to look idiotic, exhibiting the ideal of some cultures that madness and godliness are in close affinity. —Courtesy of the Bernice Pauahi Bishop Museum

(Opposite page, left) This akua hulu manu may have been the one which was sketched by John Webber and used as a lithograph illustration in the published journals of Captain Cook's third voyage. The Adam's apple is so personal a touch it seems strongly to imply a distinctive attribute of an individual. The strong anthropomorphic quality in such figures suggests the personalization of god head forms. They are in bold contrast to the great kāhili, also godly but purely abstract in form.

(Opposite page, right) The slight look of sweetness in these two akua suggest they may have been children's gods, but it does not reduce the power and ferocity pervading these figures. —Courtesy of the Bernice Pauahi Bishop Museum

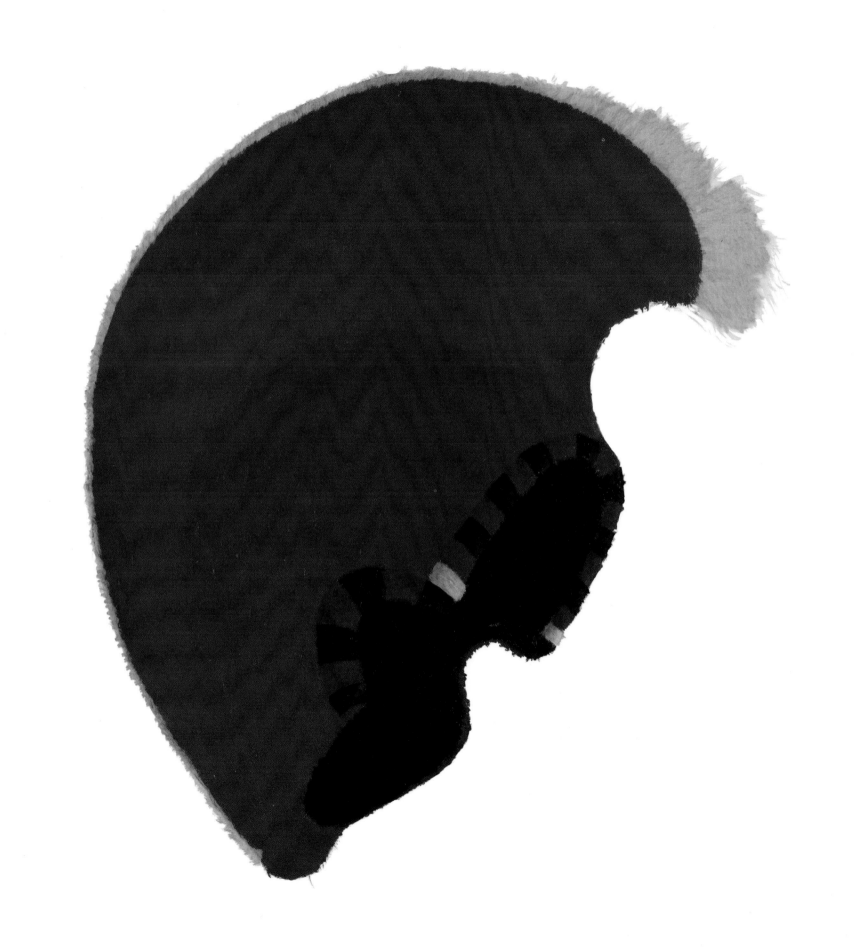

*This magnificent helmet is made from ʻiʻiwi and ʻōʻō feathers. The yellow and black feathers are from the ʻōʻō birds.*

*Red 'i'iwi and yellow mamo feathers were used in the making of this helmet.*

# Mahiole

HERE IS SOME REASON to wonder why such elaborate head gear was worn by chiefs and certain warriors in Old Hawai'i. They do not seem, upon close examination, to offer much protection from heavy spears or large rocks hurled from slings. Yet they have a look of solidity and strength. Perhaps their function was to give an appearance of invincibility or at any rate one that had a certain look of protectiveness, to the world.

There are many styles of *mahiole*. These are described at length in Dr. Buck's *Arts and Crafts of Hawai'i*. Here again another mystery is proffered. Why the differences? Why does a chief such as Boki, for example, wear the elegant, tall head piece he is wearing in the painting by Hayter, and why do we see in Miss Sarah Stone's water color studies of those in the Lever Museum so many squat tight fitting helmets fitting the head closely. These compared to Boki's magnificent head piece are scarcely less handsome. Some of them are quite exceptional in design, texture and form. This gives one the feeling that to some extent these *mahiole* were used as items of fashion.

Helmets covered the head—the *po'o kanaka*—perhaps the most revered place of the human body. Additionally, feathers, as magic collected in the depths of cold wet forests, were also able to give such protection. Feathers warded off danger or evil. In the design of a *mahiole*, especially in particular details which appear as decoration, we find markings relating to those in the *'ahu'ula?* They are not copies—not imitations—but there are markings which appear to suggest *'aumakua* and *'ohana* similar to those appearing in the *'ahu'ula*.

Sir Peter Buck divided *mahiole* into five types: "low-crested helmets, wide-crested helmets, crescent-crested helmets, hair helmets and helmets with mushroom-like ornaments"[1] but he could say little more about who wore them and why. He offers a generalized proposition that some types, "low crested" perhaps, or "crescent crested," might have been used to a greater extent or predominately on a specific island. There is no comment on the design of helmets embellished with feathers.

There must be some connection between the designs in *'ahu'ula* and *'ahuli'i* and those found in *mahiole*. Feathers—*'ō'ō, mamo, I'iwi* and black *'ō'ō*—are very carefully arranged in patterns which seem to have been carefully chosen. Some are quite simple—the magnificent surviving item which we call the Kaumuali'i helmet, for example, is made almost purely of red i'iwi feathers. In the Sarah Stone collection of water colors some helmets appear to have been made exclusively from yellow *'ō'ō* or *mamo* feathers with thin red or black lines running between the crest and that part of the helmet which fits the head.

The chiefs must have made a great appearance indeed in these regal creations, even moving the British men and officers to exclamations of awe and admiration. Early explorers wrote excitedly about Hawaiian men and their garments, and they also praised the beautiful feather *lei* worn by Hawaiian chiefesses.

[1] *Arts and Crafts of Hawai'i,* Bishop Museum, 1957

This sketch by John Webber shows one of the ways in which helmets and lei-like objects were worn together. The thick roll above the eyes is, in fact, a lei, worn to hold the helmet in place. —Courtesy of the Bernice Pauahi Bishop Museum

*This figure is said to have been the High Chief Kaiana, Kamehameha's favorite. His garments are of the finest make.*

*(Opposite page) The helmet of Ka-umu-aliʻi, the last King of Kauaʻi. It is probably the finest example of a helmet in existence.—Photo by Seth Joel, courtesy of the Bernice Pauahi Bishop Museum*

*(Below) A mushroom type mahiole base made of ʻolonā fibers. —Courtesy of the Bernice Pauahi Bishop Museum*
*(Opposite page) Mahiole from the collection of the British Museum. —Courtesy of the Bernice Pauahi Bishop Museum*

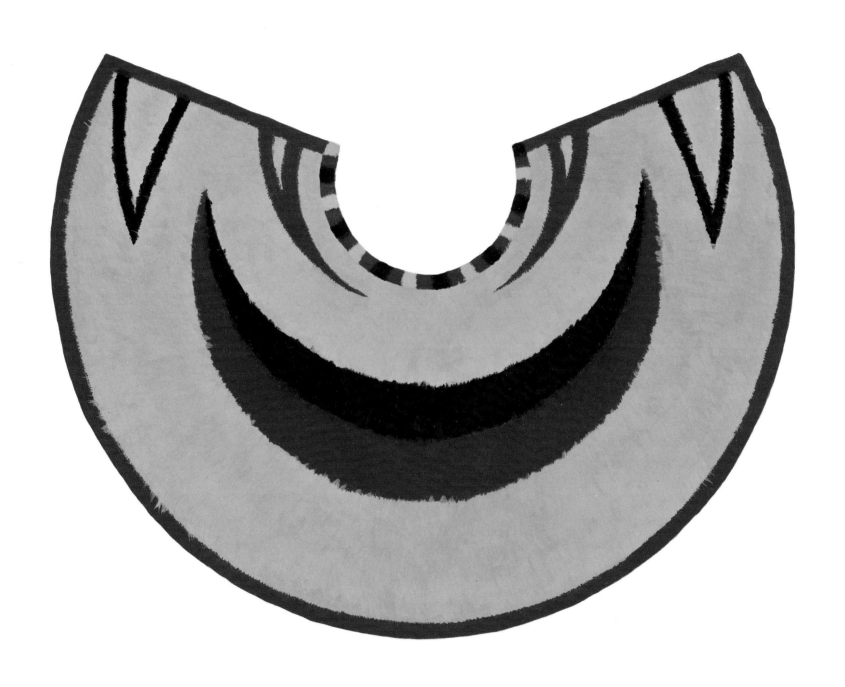

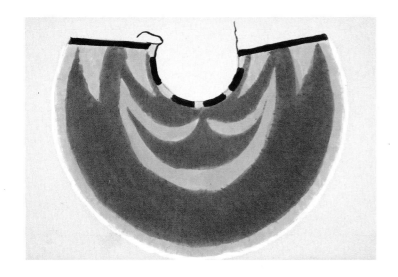
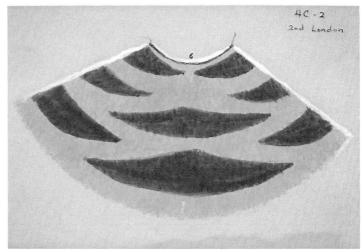

4C-2
2nd London

6

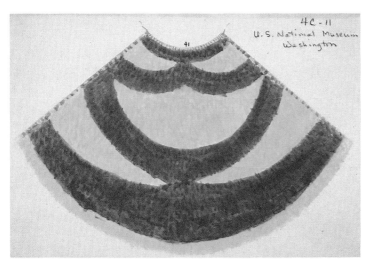
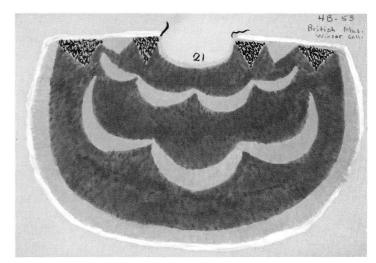

4C-11
U.S. National Museum
Washington

41

4B-53
British Mus.
Winsor coll.

21

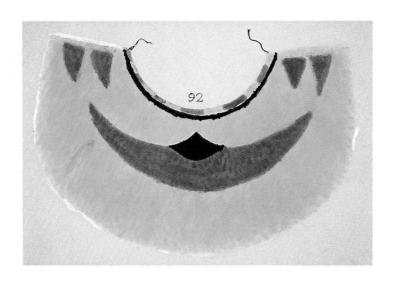
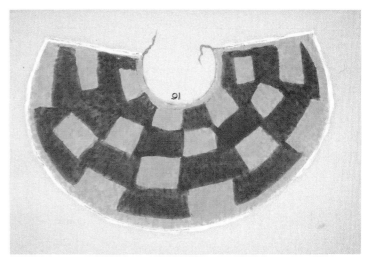

92

91

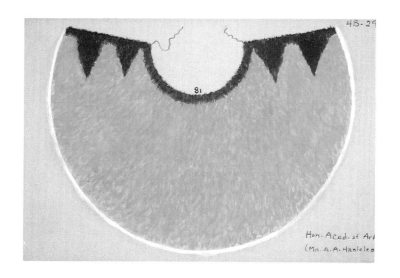

4B-29

81

Han. Acad. of Art

(Mr. A. A. Hanicle...

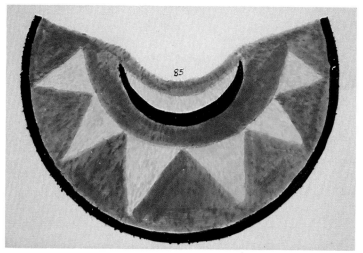

85

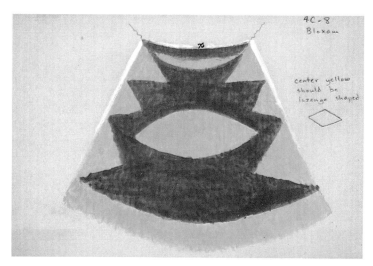

4C-8
Bloxam

76

center yellow
should be
lozenge shaped

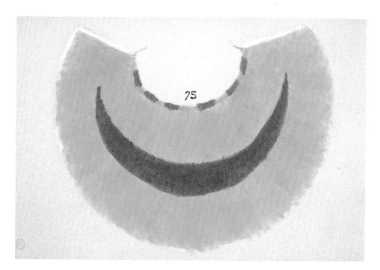

75

4C-25
Royal Scottish
Mus.

81

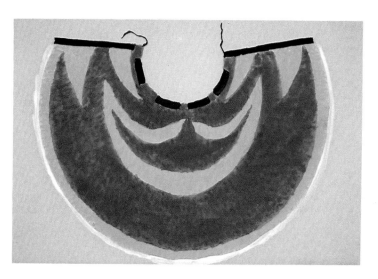

103

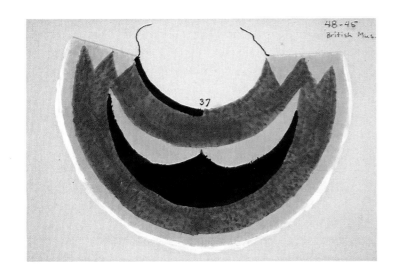

4B-46
British Mus.

37

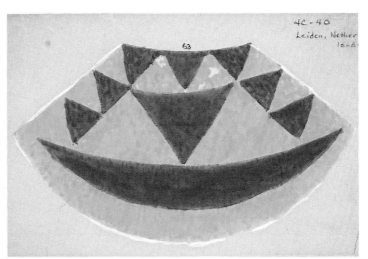

4C-40
Leiden, Netherlands

63

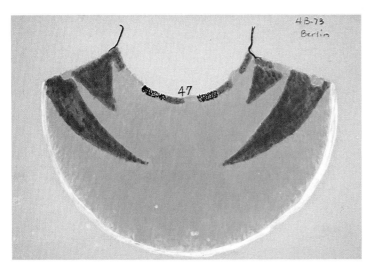

4B-73
Berlin

47

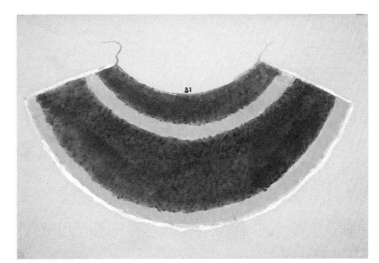

31

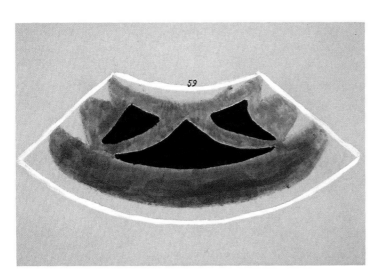

59

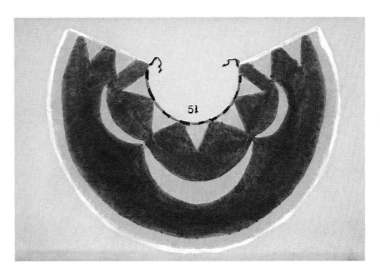

51

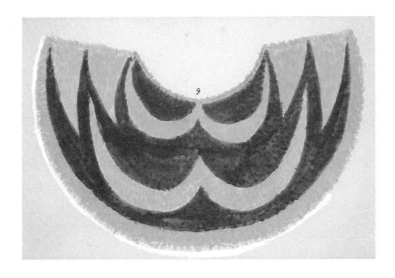

4B-28
(Mrs. A.A.
Haaleleo
Renjes
Hono.)

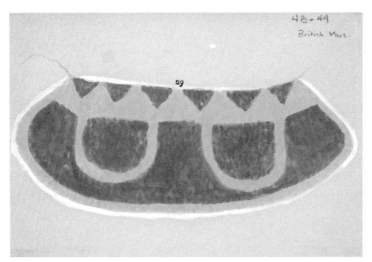

4B-49
British Mus.

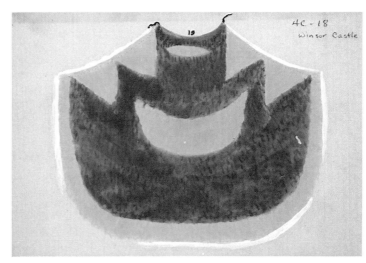

4C-18
Winsor Castle

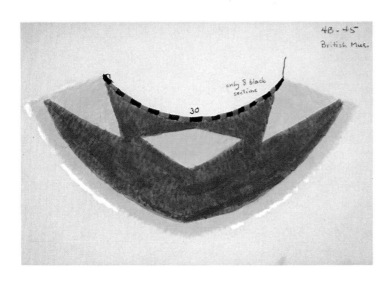

4B-45
British Mus.

only 8 black
sections

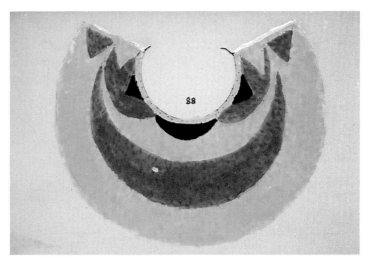

# Capes and Cloaks

OT UNTIL THE FRONT VIEWS of capes and cloaks were photographed was it understood by this writer how important design elements are to the overall appearance of feather garments. In museums, Hawaiian capes and cloaks are viewed mostly from the back. Stretched across a wall or panel they are seen in a flat, one-dimensional expanse which creates the effect of certain abstract and expressionist paintings. These magnificent creations are thus seen not so much as clothing, worn by tall, muscular men in the dazzling sunshine, but as works of art or ethnographic curiosities spread out flat on museum walls. As such, they have been denied some of their beauty. In capes and cloaks, one should study their overall—and powerful—three-dimensional reality comprised of color, texture and design. These elements seem to be lost, however, in the way they are now, for the most part, exhibited. It is as though the design elements at the front of these garments is considered unimportant, and that a more realistic vision—of a chief fully wrapped in his cape or cloak—is overlooked. What is found in the way of symbols and patterns at the back has become the decisive factor, the reason if you will, for the wearing of one of these magnificent garments.

The importance given the back view of Hawaiian feather clothing may have emerged from a notion that such garments were worn only in times of war. A chief or group of chiefs would move toward a skirmish followed by warriors who were almost magnetically drawn into battle by the sight of high chiefs, feather-wrapped in their sacred folds, moving toward the center of the fray. Here, the design at the back of the cloak would be of the ultimate importance. It graphically identified a chief in thick of battle.

The fact that kings such as Kalani-'ōpu'u, Kamehameha and other Hawai'i chiefs, as well as those of Kaua'i (including the 'O'ahu *pi'o* Chief Kaneoneo), were frequently wearing cloaks when Captain James Cook appeared makes one wonder about the strength of a theory that asserts that these were strictly garments of war, a kind of magic-charged military uniform.

The front view of feather capes and cloaks completed the total statement of *'ohana, 'aumakua* and place which was firmly planted in the esthetic destiny of the garment. In the Kiwala'ō cloak, for example, the design of the frontal area strongly differs from that of the back. The yellow triangles that meet in the area of the breast and stomach of this garment (which had been worn by this tragic young chief in the battle of Kuamo'o near Hōnaunau) are a powerful statement of *'aumakua*. Similar frontal triangles—though dramatically larger—are found in the Elgin-Kalani-'ōpu'u cloak, which possibly belonged to Kiwala'ō's father, King Kalani-'ōpu'u.[1] Four great yellow triangles—giant wings?— powerfully establish the high rank of the wearer of this garment.

Some designs could imitate tongues of fire that suggest Pele's flames and establish the *kapu moe, wela* or *wohi* of the chief wearing a garment with such designs.

In Kiwala'ō's cloak the triangles become a double row of shark's teeth, a design ele-

[1] *See Kaeppler, A., Occasional Papers, Bishop Museum. Vol. XXIV, #6. July 8, 1970. "Feather Cloaks, Ships Captains and Lords."*

*Dr. Kaeppler's exhaustive research in tracing the original ownership of this remarkably preserved cloak does not conclusively establish Kalani-'ōpu'u as its original owner. It was thought at one time to have possibly been one of the cloaks given to Captain James Cook by Kalani-'ōpu'u when the Hawaiian king visited Cook on HMS Resolution in January 1779.*

Kau-i-ke-aoūli, Kamehameha III, in a feather cape holding a kāhili lele. —Painting by William Dampier, courtesy of the Honolulu Academy of Arts

(Preceding pages) These groups of capes are from a collection of water color studies at the Bernice Pauahi Bishop Museum. There is some question about who the artist was, although it is thought to have been Sir Peter Buck, who was once the director of the Bernice Pauahi Bishop Museum. —Courtesy of the Bernice Pauahi Bishop Museum

ment cleverly established by the use of both yellow and red feathers. Again, a declaration of rank is made. The lower back of Kiwalaʻō's cloak is pure yellow—shades of things to come in the pure yellow *mamo* feathered cloak of Paiʻea Kamehameha, which is the only one of its kind in existence. In Kiwalaʻō's cloak the yellow feathered area drops from the shoulders to the ankles, there is no border at the bottom, and yellow feathers freely flow off the cloak. This generates yet another effect of status declaration and certainly strengthens the feeling that we are in the presence of a chief of *mana* rank. Oddly enough, the Kiwalaʻō garment is closer in design to Kamehameha's all yellow garment than it is to the Elgin-Kalani-ʻōpuʻu garment, which possibly belonged to Kiwalaʻō's father.

Every fragment of design—no matter how small—is of importance in the *ʻahuʻula* of Old Hawaiʻi. The material from which they are made, and the complex techniques of weaving and tying by which the feathers are fixed to their base of woven *ʻolonā* fiber, would be reason for every scrap of design to be seriously contemplated and carefully fitted into the over-all pattern before the final placement was made. But more than this, because every fragment of design was part of a chart or a prayer and represented symbolically some aspect of the wearer's life, his place in the social order, his kinship to others and his *ʻaumakua* relationships, it was important that extreme care be taken to implant feathers so that no clumsy, unplanned distortions appeared. They could augur serious trouble. There is the case of Ka-ʻōpulupulu, a famous ʻOʻahu *kahuna* who was high priest during the rule of the Maui Chief Kahahana. Kahahana became strongly attached to Ka-ʻōpulupulu and allowed the high priest to make serious decisions of state when they infringed on religion. The high priest, for example, would not allow King Kahekili of Maui (who had set up Kahahana's rule of ʻOʻahu) to be given the rights to collect whale ivory on ʻOʻahu beaches. He also encouraged Kahahana to discourage the use of certain *heiau* in the Koʻolaupoko area.

To seek revenge, Kahekili had the sacred feather *malo* of Kahahana copied by feather makers on Maui. To do this, these feather makers sneaked into the place where the *malo* was hidden, and where it was in the care of Ka-ʻōpulupulu, the only person who knew the intricacies of its design and making. But although the Maui-made *malo* was a skillfully copied imitation, it was not perfect. In order to alienate Kaʻōpulupulu from Kahahana, Kahekili brought out the imitation *malo* whilst the ʻOʻahu regent was on a visit to Maui. Enraged to think that his faithful *kahuna* had allowed the sacred *malo* to be taken, Kahahana returned to ʻOʻahu, tracked Kaʻōpulupulu to the Waiʻanae coast and ordered him taken. In order to return the magic of the Kahekili's treachery Kaʻōpulupulu walked into the sea and drowned himself.

Kahekili knew that the power locked in the feathers of Kahahana's *malo* were charged with *mana,* and that if they were misused—despite the ruse of copying the original—disaster could strike (from the unpublished notebooks of Gertrude MacKinnon Damon).

Color was skillfully used to place emphasis on one feature or another. Black feathers,

for example, were of paramount importance in one garment because of some aspects of a person's ancestry. Red or yellow feathers would have a similar purpose in yet other garments, and place of birth, or one's participation in certain events, might also be registered by color, if not by pattern. The *'ahu'ula* of Old Hawai'i are in fact remarkable testaments of garments designed for specific people. Each garment was unique and carried the highly personalized message of a person's ancestral and kinship connections, his *'aumakua* relationships and other special features which might register important and known facts about a particular person.

The remarkable balance in the areas of red and black feathers found in the Kapi'olani-nui cape, including the "balanced" feeling in the space occupied by yellow feathers, tell us something about this interesting chiefess. Because it is known to have been her garment, worn by her on occasion, one is led to believe it was a post-Cook creation, made perhaps during her lifetime. She was known to have been a person we would consider today as adjusted—a "put-together" person without too much conflict. Kamakau has written about her in some detail, and from his and other writings we have learned that Kapi'olani adapted extremely well to the changes that came to Hawai'i after Captain Cook. In her home, for example, she cultivated the arts of home-making like a skilled New England homemaker. Indeed, people would walk past her house in Hilo simply to see and to smell the wonders of New England baking—breads, pies, cakes—which she would place in the windows of her kitchen for cooling. Or as Kamakau writes:

> Ka-pi'o-lani was like the foreigners, and the duties of a foreign (*haole*) women were those that she undertook. She and the girls of her household were adept in mixing bread dough, in baking bread, cake, making rolls, soups, frying, and the preparation of all kinds of foods. Her table was laden with the food of the foreigners.
>
> Her household was well kept. The attire of the women was neat and tidy and resembled that of the foreigners. Those who waited on the table wore dresses (*pukikī*). She constantly wore dresses as well as linen *holokus* of all kinds. She was comparable to a foreign woman . . . .
>
> —Kamakau, S., *Ruling Chiefs of Hawaii* pp 382-383

So was the first Kapi'olani described by someone close to being a contemporary. She was Kapi'olani from the Big Island; her father was Keawe-mauhili, a chief of great rank, the half-brother of King Kalani-'ōpu'u. She learned English very quickly, she learned to cook—*haole* style—and she became a quite thoroughly acculturated and devout Christian. She even went down one time to the pit, to Kilauea caldera, to defy Pele. She called to Pele to come and consume her. It was quite a theatrical exercise.

*These three cloaks demonstrate three very different and strong elements in design. Each makes a definitive statement about itself and its wearer. No one would mistake the wearers of these garments, one from the other. —Photo by Ben Patnoi, courtesy of the Bernice Pauahi Bishop Museum*

*A collar fragment that was once probably part of an old cloak. —Photos courtesy of the Bernice Pauahi Bishop Museum*

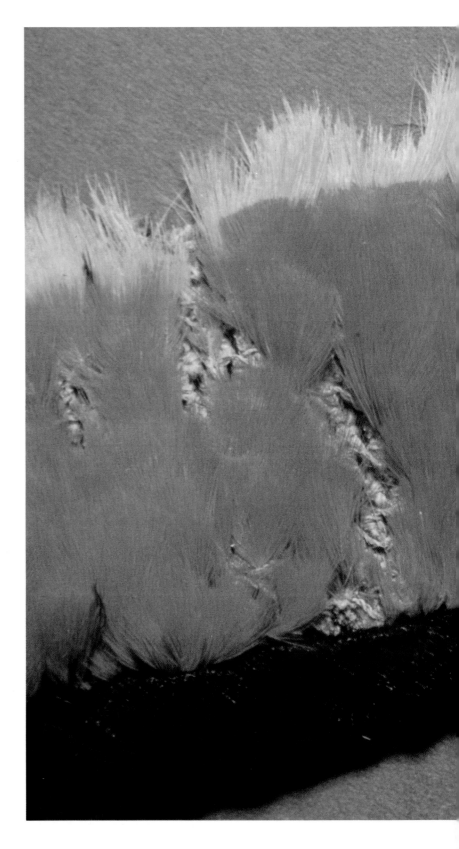

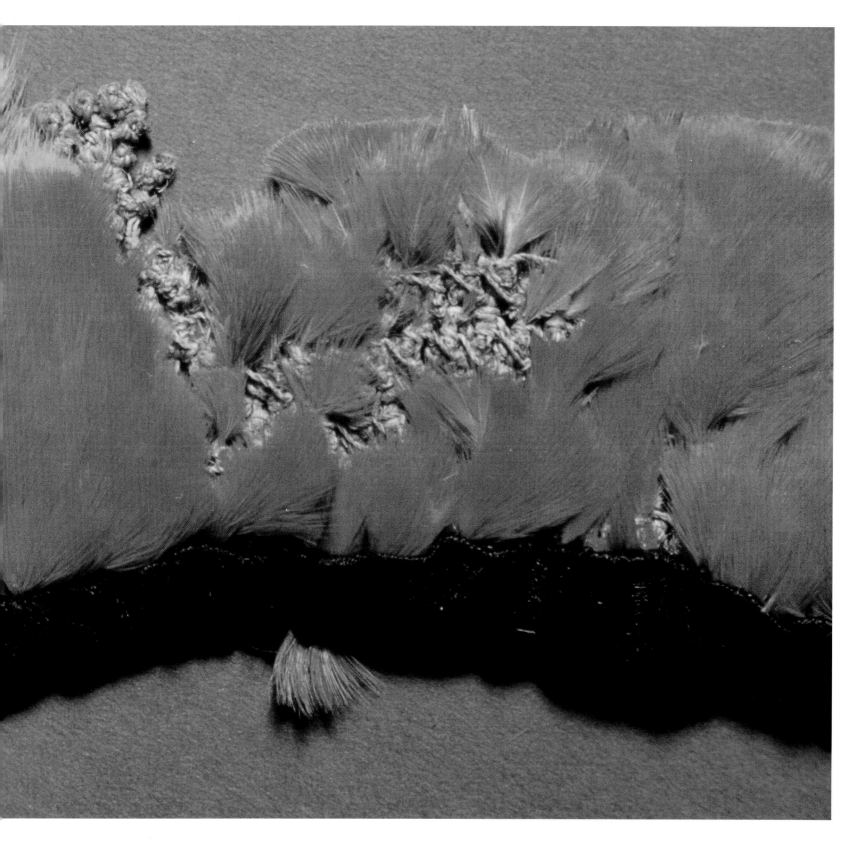

# Notes: The Kiwala'ō Cloak

The Kiwala'ō cloak has a special poignance for me because of what I think was the rather sad, ineffectual life of its owner. He didn't rise and shine to the degree that Kamehameha did and he strikes me as being a pathetic character among the dramatic and accomplished personae of late 18th Century Hawaiian history. The fact that his cloak has survived and is presently in the Bernice Pauahi Bishop Museum collection (and is occasionally put out on exhibit) is a comforting statement of survival. His memory is alive, but it unfortunately brings to my mind the reality that he did not amount to very much. His death at Kuamo'o during the first battle, the *VERY FIRST BATTLE* of the wars of conquest, was a minor tragedy of Hawaiian history with pathetic overtones of futility and ineptitude. For all of its beauty, Kiwala'ō's cloak evokes the failures of his short life and was indicative of his being almost doomed to die—and to die nobly, wearing his magnificent cloak and his *lei niho palaoa* which was torn from his neck by Ke'eaumoku, the father of Queen Ka'ahumanu. He took it as a prize of war. That was written down by Hawaiian historians later.

Brigham tells us that the Kiwala'ō cloak was placed over the Queen's throne on public occasions, and, of course, it can still be seen from time to time. The cloak seems to have been made from the ruins of many other garments. The length is 60 inches, the width at the base is 144 inches, and the *nae* is composed of more than 30 pieces. *Nae* is the thatching—the matting or net structure—to which feathers are attached.

Although the Kiwala'ō cloak may not be the most outstanding of Hawaiian cloaks, it is in fairly good shape. Probably the fact that it was pieced together in the sennit underpinnings has something to do with its age and value. The whole idea of *mana*—the spiritual power—collected in made things was related strongly to the age factor; very old and very ancient things had more *mana* than very new things which were too young to have acquired a desired richness of *mana* absorbable only through time. So, if a cloak was not brand new—perfect in its fitting or in its appearance, but aged—it probably had a great deal of spiritual clout.

Kiwala'ō was the son of Kalani-'ōpu'u, which made him the highest ranking chief of his generation on the island of Hawai'i. He was also the son of Kalola, the sister of Kahekili of Maui. She was the ranking *pi'o*—even higher than her brother Kahekili, because she was the eldest in the family. So, Kiwala'ō, between his parents, inherited tremendous rank, the highest rank of Maui, the highest rank of Hawai'i, and the highest rank of 'O'ahu. Kalani-'ōpu'u's mother, Kiwala'ō's grandmother, was a *pi'o* chiefess of 'O'ahu. This is how Kalani-'ōpu'u got his name. Kalani-'ōpu'u, the chief with the bud, *'ōpu'u.* This was the small whale tooth which was worn by 'O'ahu chiefs. It was uncarved, unlike the big *niho palaoa* which is carved into a hoop-like form that collected *mana* for its wearer. Kalani-'ōpu'u reveals his 'O'ahu connection in wearing his *niho 'ōpu'u.* He was also part Hawai'i royalty. Kamaka'imoku of Ka'ū was his grandmother. He was also an Alapa'i, a nephew of Alapa'i *nui,* a son of Alapa'i's brother. So, in terms of birth, there is no getting away from Kiwala'ō's importance. His right to succession on the island of

*(Opposite page) This cloak was made for and worn by the ali'i nui, Kiwala'ō of Hawai'i. He was wearing this cloak when he was mortally struck down in the battle of Kuamo'o. The stunning finish of red 'i'iwi feathers, which outlines half circles of yellow at the shoulder, gracefully accents the remaining royal mass of yellow which falls to the ankles and is a statement of rank. The front view of the cloak has five rows of sharks teeth which register 'aumakua and 'ohana connections. —Photo by Ben Patnoi, courtesy of the Bernice Pauahi Bishop Museum*

Hawai'i was beyond dispute. It isn't quite clear what was wrong with him. Some early informants said that he was weak physically, that he was effeminate, and that, alongside of Kamehameha (they were the same age), he was pathetic. They were almost the same rank, especially if we take the view that Kahekili was Kamehameha's father.

This brings us to the *heiau* at Pākini between Ka'ū and Kahuku. The Kahuku district of Ka'ū on the Big Island, up on the high slopes of the South Point, spreads out in a fan along the slopes of Mauna Loa. There had been a high chief, 'Imaka-koloa of the great Hilo clan of 'I, who had been subversive. He had been working against Kalani-'ōpu'u and had devised a plan to unseat the old king. He wanted to elevate the 'I's once again to the command of the Big Island of Hawai'i. He was eventually tracked down and caught in the Puna area, then taken to Pākini Heiau located above South Point or Kalae in the Kahuku region of Ka'ū.

There, 'Imaka-koloa was prepared for sacrifice. The ritual celebration of this event was to take place at Pākini, a *luakini* type *heiau* where human sacrifices following battle were performed. The *kahuna* and the chiefs decided, for reasons unknown to us, that this important event should take place at Ka'ū, and so the sacrifice of 'Imaka-koloa was elaborately laid out. Special ceremonies would also be performed, celebrating the coming of age of Kiwala'ō and Kamehameha. It was an event of the first importance. Two princes of very high rank primed for consecration and the corpse of a high chief provided a perfect human combination for the performance of these rites. Pākini, on the cool slopes of Kahuku where the winds blew in a lively fashion down to the sea, was a perfect *mise en scene*.

In the ritual of this event, the heir apparent was given the job of lifting the dead body of sacrifice onto the *lele,* the platform upon which a corpse was placed. There it sat until the body decomposed, then the flesh was burned off and the bones saved.

When this important ceremony took place, both young chiefs were probably decked out in their best feather cloaks. Kiwala'ō was probably wearing the one we have pictured. It was probably the most important occasion during which he wore this cloak.

There are, however, conflicting reports. The Hawaiian reports which come from the old newspapers are very graphically written.

During the sacrifice of 'Imaka-koloa, for example, certain unusual circumstances took place. For one thing, he had been killed before the day of this ceremony in which Kamehameha and Kiwala'ō were participating. One Hawaiian informant wrote that the corpse was absolutely stinking when the ceremony took place and it was very difficult for the chiefs and the *kahuna* to sit there and wait for it to be lifted onto the *lele*. Also, tradition has it that Kamehameha, in order to gain *mana* and to get used to the smell, spent the night with the corpse, anticipating that he might have to do something in the ritual to complete it if Kiwala'ō failed. The corpse was almost seven feet long, and must have weighed a great deal; on top of the dead weight was the stench. For some reason Kiwala'ō could not lift the corpse of 'Īmaka-koloa and place it atop the *lele,* and when Kiwala'ō failed, Kamehameha moved in, lifted the body and easily put it on the *lele*. This caused a furor among the gathered chiefs. Kamehameha's uncle, Kalani-'ōpu'u (who really adored him) was reported to have said he had done the wrong thing. He said: "It looks to the gathered chiefs that you are reaching out for more power and that they see your act of lifting 'Īmaka-koloa as sort of an appeal to the gods to grant you more than you have been given. I have given you care of the god, Kū-kā'ili-moku, and there is your power." Rule of the land had been given to Kiwala'ō—Kamehameha had been put in charge of caring for the family gods, as had chiefs who were second in line for many generations among Hawaiians.

Was someone other than Kamehameha supposed to move in and lift the body and place it on the *lele* at Pākini? It seems to me that Kamehameha did an impulsive thing, but that it was done in the interest of protecting the ritual from being contaminated because of Kiwala'ō's failure to perform his part properly. Was this act that of a self-seeker or a statesman? According to tradition, the *kahuna* and chiefs were much disturbed over what took place. They saw bad omens in the way the ceremony ended. Less than a year later the old king was dead and Kamehameha and Kiwala'ō were at war.

Well, we've digressed far from Kiwala'ō's feather cloak, but since Brigham, who is the chief informant to date on cloaks, tells us that Kamehameha slew Kiwala'ō, some of this lore had to be recalled.

Unfortunately, the two young men were contemporaries; they were practically the same age, but one was powerful, aggressive and already a brilliant warrior-statesman. The other was not. He was probably a poet or meant for the priesthood. We don't know much about Kiwala'ō's personal life. I believe he might have busied himself with making feather *lei* and being concerned with some of the more artistic pursuits of the culture. He simply was not a warrior, not a fighter, not a leader of that time—and he failed! He died! The people that were surrounding and helping the stronger of the two men managed to maneuver Kiwala'ō into the position where he was one of the first victims of wars of conquest that began after the death of Kalani-'ōpu'u in 1781.

*The Joy cloak with its yellow circles floating in a sky of red packs less psychic wallop than most of the great feather cloaks of old Hawai'i. It is decorative and playful. The yellow circles dominate the back, even to the finish of half-circles at the neck. In the front view, triangular teeth or abstract wings fall in two rows from top to bottom. — Photo by Ben Patnoi, courtesy of the Bernice Pauahi Bishop Museum*

# Notes: The Joy Cloak

I'm sketching the Joy cloak at the Bishop Museum, where it is presently on exhibition. It is hanging very nicely with another cloak which is slightly smaller. The Joy cloak is famous for its circles. It is one of two surviving cloaks in which circles are used as an element of design. Circles of *mamo* and *'ō'ō* feathers flow in neat rows across the cloak. There are seven circles in the bottom row, gradually dwindling to three at the topmost row. These are similar to the semi-circles at the neck of the Kiwala'ō cloak. It is possible that the Joy cloak was worn by a chief who walked in a parade through Boston streets. Adrienne Kaeppler reported on an onlooker who saw him walking there in 1785 or 1787. There is no definite knowledge of who this chief was, but he was called Attoo and he must have been quite a sight, wearing both a helmet and a cloak. It was given as a gift to Captain Joy of the Joy family, a Boston family of merchants, who used the feather cloak as a knee rug for sleigh rides. They gave it finally to the Boston Museum of Fine Arts, where it was on display for a long, long time. It eventually came home to Hawai'i, and is now happily here and happily on exhibit. Certainly one of the most unusual looking cloaks—by virtue of its circles—the Joy *'ahu'ula* would be exceptional in any collection. The circle is not the most popular form in Polynesian art, and it appears rarely.

In the Joy *'ahu'ula* there are three half circles at the top, on each side of the neck in front, and at the back, which resemble those we have seen in the Kiwala'o *'ahu'ula*. The red mass in the background of the Joy cloak, filled with circles, had a definite meaning. Wearers, and wearers' associates, and I am sure some of the populace as well, who saw it worn in the Hawaiian environment could recognize distinct signs encompassing the three fundamental elements found in designs of *'ahu'ula*, i.e. *'aumakua*, *'ohana* and rank. Again we have the sharp-pointed, finlike pyramidical shapes at the front of the garment, which also resemble massive teeth, especially shark teeth. What are the circles? Stars? Or do they represent people? Families? People in a family of the chief who wore this cloak? Ancestors? A cluster of them? We have thirteen, eighteen, twenty-two circles—three half-circles. What do they represent? Does it matter? Is it important? Are they simply circles? They make a very pretty design in this particular cloak, but they also make a statement concerning rank, *'ohana* and *'aumakua*. It is worth noting that in the design of the red *'i'iwi* section of the cloak, when it is observed spread out on a wall, there appears a great curve at the bottom with two sharp angular ends, reminding one of a boat of early making, like a Venetian or an Egyptian vessel, with the circles looking like windows in the decks above. Because there were so many windows and so many decks it suggests Noah's Ark. All of the windows for air and for light and for whatever else. But it only has this look when it is spread out.

The Joy cloak forces out of us many kinds of reactions and it creates a number of images. Why does something as simple as that red mass in the middle, filled with its yellow circles that run from one end to the other, evoke so many pictures for us—so many images. The more you look at these garments—the more you realize that, although some of the designs are extremely simple, and ordinary—the more you realize that they are actually greatly complex and artistically inspired, telling us much about the old culture. Their makers must have imagined what would happen, and what did happen, when the garments were completed and when they were seen by the public for the first time. Worn where the populace could see and react to what they were seeing, they must have evoked lively comments on the design which had been so carefully placed into the predominant pattern of feathers of this garment with its tantalizing yellow circles.

Much thought would have been given to the colors and the combinations of kinds of feathers. Why this form in the design would be black and not yellow, or, vice versa, or why in fact so much more of one color was used instead of another. To this very day these ancient garments tease the imagination and tempt us to dig ever deeper for understanding the meaning of these works of art in terms of their social, political, philosophical and spiritual emphasis.

The front view of the Elgin-Kalani-ʻōpuʻu cloak, which possibly belonged to King Kalani-ʻōpuʻu of Hawaiʻi. There are four great triangles that abstractly suggest wings or giant feathers—a variation of those found on his son Kiwalaʻōʻs cloak. The rear view of the cloak shows the importance of the great yellow "V". It plunges into a mass of red, which is flecked with tiny yellow spots—suggesting stars—and is finished at the ankles with a band of yellow. There are subtle connections between this superb cloak and the one worn by Kiwalaʻō. —Photo by Ben Patnoi, courtesy of the Bernice Pauahi Bishop Museum

# Notes: The Elgin-Kalani-'ōpu'u Cloak

The Elgin-Kalani-'ōpu'u is a HUGE cloak, one of the largest in existence. It has little flecks of yellow in the red feathers that are like spring flowers sprouting from a field. There is a sharp triangle that falls upside down from the shoulders to the middle of the back, coming to a very sharp point at the bottom. This massive triangle is of yellow feathers and the area into which it falls is of red feathers. The design of the red occupies almost the whole of the back. The only thing that you see from the back, if it were worn, would be a mass of red with this upside down triangle or pyramid falling dramatically into the middle of the back. At the bottom of the cloak there is a wide border of yellow feathers, probably *mamo.* It's a strikingly beautiful cloak, and might well have belonged to a chief as important as Kalani-'ōpu'u who was the reigning *ali'i nui* or *ali'i 'ai moku,* the "King" of the island of Hawai'i when Captain Cook arrived.

But, there again, this design is less suggestive of elements of the *'aumakua*—the mystical. It is plainer. The red area seems to have been implanted in the yellow, but put where it is strictly for design purposes. It might not be as spiritual and mystical in its looks as some of the others, but it is handsome indeed in its earthly aspects. And, as an earthly thing, it doesn't assault your brain or strain it too hard to figure out what the design is all about. To have to search in your spirit, in your heart, to feel really what the garment tries to tell us, is not so true of this cloak. Feathers and the coloration, the size of it, the hang of it, all come together wonderfully.

Captain James Cook wrote about Kalani-'ōpu'u and his cloaks:

At noon, Tareopu'u, [i.e., Kalani-'ōpu'u] in a large canoe, attended by two others, set out from the village and paddled to the ships in great state. In the first canoe was Tareopu'u, in the second Koa—with four images, the third was filled with hogs and vegetables. As they went along, those in the center canoe kept singing with much solemnity, from which we concluded that this procession had some of their religious ceremonies mixed with it. But instead of going on board, they came on our side; their appearance was very grand. The chiefs standing up, dressed in their cloaks and caps. And in the center canoe were the busts of what we supposed their gods made of basketwork, variously covered with red, black, white, and yellow feathers. The eyes represented by a bit of pearl oyster shell with a black button. And the teeth were those of dogs, the mouths of all were strangely distorted, as well as other features. We drew out our little guard to receive him and the captain, observing the king, went on shore, followed him. After we had gotten into the marquee, the king got up and threw, in a graceful manner over the captain's shoulders, the cloak he himself wore and put a feathered cap on his head and a very handsome fly flap in his hand, besides which he laid down at the captain's feet, five or six cloaks more—all very beautiful and, to them, of the greatest value. His attendant brought large hogs with other refreshments which were also presented.

—from Beaglehole, p. 512

It is not surprising that Captain Cook was given splendid cloaks by Kalani-'ōpu'u. Cook, after all, was thought to be the God Lono. One of the reasons he was honored as the God Lono was that he arrived in Hawai'i at the time of the *Makahiki,* a celebration which took place in the winter months of the year. The other was that like the God Lono he was fair-skinned.

These magnificent cloaks were set at his feet, one put on his shoulders with a helmet by Kalani-'ōpu'u himself, who was described by Captain Samwell as being very tall and very thin and, he thought, emaciated as a result of habitually drinking *'awa.* His skin had the appearance of peeling off, which left a fairness, or a blotchy fairness on his skin.

For a time it was called the Kalani-'ōpu'u cloak, and that was its title when it first came home to Hawai'i in 1968. But it is also known as the Elgin cloak because it was collected by Lord Elgin on October 1, 1792. We are not absolutely sure that it was Kalani-'ōpu'u's cloak, but the dating of events involved in its exchange from one person to the next suggests that it might have belonged to King Kalani-'ōpu'u of Hawai'i and that it might have been the very garment which he placed on the shoulders of Captain James Cook during the same Kealakekua Bay ceremonies we have just described. On its journey to London, possession of this fine cloak went to another sea captain somewhere in Southeast Asia. From there it changed hands again and eventually fell into the possession of a member of the Bruce family, a younger cousin of Lord Elgin. The cloak and a feather helmet were ultimately acquired by Lord Elgin and were placed in the family seat of the Bruces in Scotland. Lord Elgin would hang it and store it intermittently. A magnificent box or container was made to provide a repository for both the cloak and the helmet. When it was sold to the Bishop Museum in the 1960s and returned to Hawai'i it was in beautiful condition. It is now the featured object in one of the museum's exhibits and is considered a prime example of old Hawaiian featherwork.

# Notes: The Kintore Cloak

Another magnificent cloak very worthy of study is the Kintore Cloak, a cloak which was given this name because for many years it hung on the walls of Keith Hall, home of the Earls of Kintore in Scotland. We know nothing of the origins of this magnificent ʻahuʻula. For whom was it made? When was it made? Why the use of plain lines, we ask, as we have asked why the circles in the Joy cloak.

The ancients have left us baffled—both the British adventurers who collected the first of the Hawaiian treasures resting now in the world's leading museums and the Hawaiian ancients who traded or gave these Hawaiian works of art to the first visitors to come to Hawaii. Why were they—on both sides—so reluctant to give information concerning the vital statistics of the feather cloaks and capes. Who made them? Who wore them? What were the implications, religious and social, in the designs?

Nothing of this kind was reported or written down. The journal keepers of Captain Cook's ship's companies usually wrote down meticulous details of their encounters and transactions with the Hawaiian people. Lieutenant King even wrote a list of words and compared meaning and spelling with equivalent usage by Tongans and Tahitians, and he also wrote a detailed genealogy of the ruling families, which was quite accurate but not inclusive.

But no one took the time or effort to write down details of Hawaiian featherwork. Who made them? What did the designs imply? When were the garments worn? I should think the English sailors who collected featherwork articles to take home would have been struck by their beauty, elegance and artistry enough to want to know who made them and why, and who wore them and why. There is not a word of this kind in the journals.

Lord Byron (Captain George Anson) who succeeded his cousin in the famed post of this title, was commissioned by the British government in 1824 to return the bodies of King Kamehameha II and his consort, Queen Kamāmalu, to the Sandwich Islands. The King and Queen had contracted measles in London and died, much to the distress and puzzlement of the British people and much to the sorrow of the subjects of the royal couple, the native people of *Hawaiʻi nei.* Byron, as commander of the HMS *Blonde,* returned the bodies of the King and Queen safely to their native home and was received with enthusiasm by the people. In Byron's company were a number of young aristocratic Englishmen, among them the Honorable Mr. Keith, son of the Earl of Kintore. Byron and his officers traded furiously in Hawaiian ethnographic objects, especially feather capes and cloaks, and had been given the unheard of privilege of taking what they chose from the sacred temple of Hale-o-Keawe at Hōnaunau. "Therefore when the *Blonde* sailed away from Hawaiian waters," anthropologist Adrienne Kaeppler writes, "she carried a cargo of featherwork probably second only to that of Captain Cook. . . .". The acquisition of the garment which has come to be known as the Kintore cloak has been traced with admirable precision by Mrs. Kaeppler, who writes:

*(Opposite page) The parallel lines of the Kintore cloak seem to make a statement about time in the infinite far reaches of the universe. During the early voyages of migration, Hawaiian navigators sedulously observed the swells in the ocean and the stars in the wide, open heaven above to guide them to their new home. The hued lines of this cloak speak of unseen forces powerful and pervading—a profound source of mana and inspiration. The making of this cloak was probably the work of dedicated mystics. —Photo by Ben Patnoi, courtesy of the Bernice Pauahi Bishop Museum*

William Keith, the third son of the seventh Earl of Kintore (ninth Lord Falconer of Halkerton), . . . accompanied Lord Byron on May 7 to the official reception given by the Hawaiian king (Kamehameha III, . . . On this occasion, the gifts from King George IV of England were presented. We are not told what was given by the Hawaiians in return, but judging from other gifts exchanges, we can assume that feather cloaks were included, and perhaps it was at this time that another we cannot say for sure—but Mr. Keith went home to Scotland with one of the most beautiful pieces of featherwork ever produced.

—Bernice Pauahi Bishop Museum—Occasional Papers XXIV, 1970, p. 94

This important cloak found its way to Keith Hall in Aberdeenshire, home of the Earls of Kintore, where it was placed in a specially made glass-fronted case which hung on the wall of the fourth floor landing where it remained for 140 years.

Dr. Kaeppler writes of the exact place in which the cloak was displayed.

The cloak was lined with cloth and displayed in a specially built case on the fourth floor top landing of a beautiful open staircase. Subdued natural light from a frosted skylight illuminated the brilliant red, yellow, and black feathers. Here it remained for some 140 years in an honored place, surrounded by portraits of the Kintore family and other illustrious persons, passing in a direct line from one earl to the next.

The more recent destiny of the Kintore cloak has been documented as well by Dr. Kaeppler.

The eleventh Earl, however had no son, and in 1928 he wrote to a representative of Bishop Museum, "If circumstances ever permitted there is nothing that would give me greater pleasure than being able to present it to the Bishop Museum." In 1969 this wish was carried out by his widow, Helena, Countess of Kintore, in recognition of the 80th anniversary of Bishop Museum. The cloak was formerly known as the Lord Falconer Cloak, because at the time of the 1928 correspondence the eleventh Earl held the title of Lord Falconer. However, it is now known as the Kintore Cloak.

—Bernice Pauahi Bishop Museum—Occasional Papers XXIV, 1970, pp. 94 & 95

In summing up her thoughts regarding the Kintore Cloak, Dr. Kaeppler comments on the use of lines in the design and the singular use of the color black.

1. *Force & Force —Art & Artifacts of the 18th Century – p. 53*

The cloak is remarkably well preserved, owing, perhaps, to its lining, to the closed case in which it was kept, and probably to infrequent handling. It was not traded through several hands before reaching Keith Hall, Scotland. It is 58 inches long and 88 inches wide, and is the only known cloak that is striped horizontally in red, yellow, and black. Each piece of Hawaiian featherwork is, in fact, unique. However, some design elements are found on many pieces with only light variations and their uniqueness lies in the combination of elements. The usual design elements are triangles, crescents, and lozenges, but narrow stripes of this kind are exceedingly rare. The Kintore Cloak is also unique in that it is the only one in which large elements of black are introduced into the body of the cloak design."

—Bernice Pauahi Bishop Museum—Occasional Papers XXIV, 1970, pp. 95 & 96

It is a great piece of luck that the unusual Kintore Cloak has come home to Hawai'i and is now a treasured article of Hawaiian featherwork art in the permanent collection of the Bernice Pauahi Bishop Museum.

Looking at the cloak, what of these parallel lines? Sarah Stone painted an *'ahu'ula* in the Lever Museum made up only of yellow and red lines alternating in equal lengths for the full length of the garment.[1] Once again lines. But once again different. No two capes or cloaks are exactly alike. Each seems to had been made to suit a specific individual in terms of *'ohana, 'aumakua* and rank. We know from Sarah Stone's water color of the red and yellow—lined cloak that at least another piece of Hawaiian featherwork art used parallel lines as the *modus vivendi* for its design.

These lines, especially as they come together at the front of the cloak, are wonderfully abstract. In the realistic sense they suggest horizons and waves, winds and clouds. In more abstract terms they seem to speak to me as lines which make a point about time and space, as though the makers or wearers were priests who dealt in abstract terms with the universe and recorded this in the extraordinarily beautiful design of the garment we call the Kintore Cloak.

The yellow mass of thousands of mamo feathers in this royal garment belonging to King Kamehameha seem to speak of his unique position. The declaration of royal status is obvious in the use of only yellow feathers—especially mamo, the rarest of all. The total lack of design suggests that he was beyond the need of symbols to declare his human status. He was too close to the gods to be in need of the usual markings of rank. The total use of yellow also may have been another way Kamehameha established his relationship between the royal chiefs of 'O'ahu's pi'o rank and his mother's 'O'ahu ancestors, who for nine generations were the products of brother-sister marriages. —Photo by Ben Patnoi, courtesy of the Bernice Pauahi Bishop Museum

In this grouping of cloaks belonging to Kiwalaʻō (left), Kalani-ʻōpuʻu (center), and Kamehameha (right), the importance of yellow is established. The plunging of the Elgin-Kalani-ʻōpuʻu seems to connect in an almost evolutionary way to the bold expanses of rare mamo feathers in the garments which belonged to Kalani-ʻōpuʻu's son and heir, Kiwalaʻō, and to his nephew, Paiea Kamehameha. They were the highest chiefs of their time, equalled in rank only by the senior branch of the Piʻilani family of Maui. Grouped as they are, these three garments speak for the authority of the rank of the men who wore them. —Photo by Ben Patnoi, courtesy of the Bernice Pauahi Bishop Museum

# Notes: The Steen Bille Cape

The Steen Bille Cape is striking because of its color combinations. Green and yellow alone are used, with the stronger yellow in the background. Again, we observe crescents. Around the neck we have green crescents bent inwards almost to touch each other at the nape of the neck. Then other crescents, lower down in the front and not bent. They are straight, erect pyramids. The middle crescent in back has a slight pyramidal rising in the center, a lovely shape for this particular composition. It fits wonderfully, it seems to me. The little pyramid in the middle, reaching out almost to touch the encircling crescent around the neck.

The rich yellow, the rich greens, the little touches of black around the neck, the one yellow spot at the nape, and then red, black and green down the front demand attention. I have a strong feeling that the artist in this case has a certain delicacy, a certain gentleness of spirit, but there again are the half crescents. I don't see why we should avoid using the metaphor of the fin because the shark is so important in the life of the Hawaiians, after all, at the highest point he was 'aumakua. Most Hawaiian families that I know have claimed the shark as their 'aumakua. Whether they're accurate or not in this claim, I don't know— but they do claim it. If you were to get close to this, you would see how it would be. It would be a fin-like thing. The fantasy of them closing in around the neck, touching these, distorting the shape of the pair of fins. I think that it is delicate and it is strong—it has great appeal. It has stronger appeal than some of the older, wilder, more mystical 'ahu which are heavy and powerful. They are sort of aching with philosophy and religion. But this one is light and gay and there's a gentleness in it. It is pretty.

It was probably worn by a chief of very special qualities—a chief of strong esthetic sensibilities who perhaps also had very special family connections whose details have been lost to us in the dimness of time past. I'm glad that it exists. It is still in Copenhagen, but maybe someday it will come home. So far, no capes or cloaks of green feathers are still extant in Hawai'i.

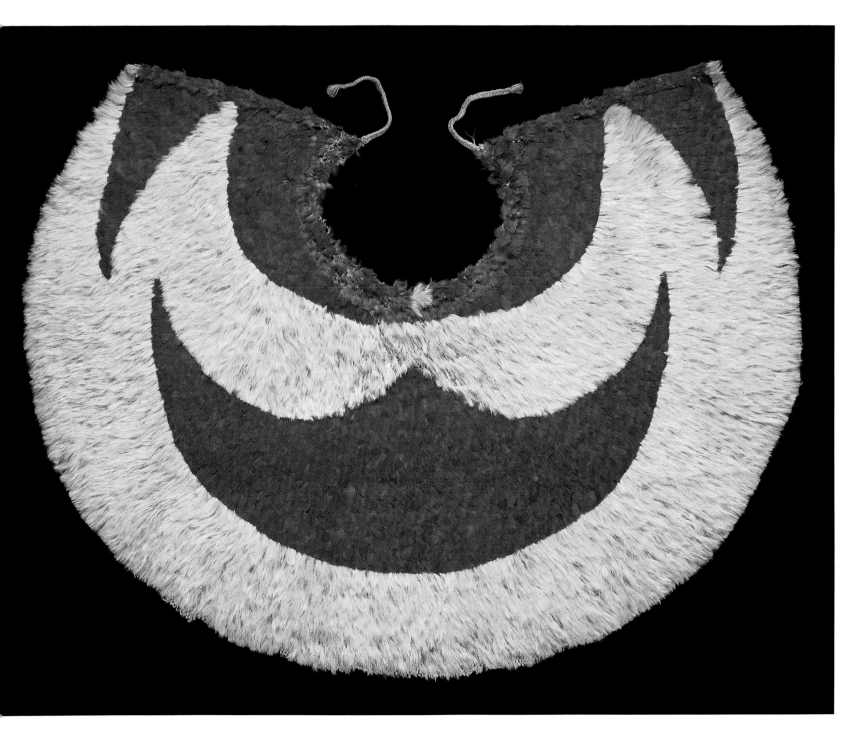

This 'ahuli'i made from the feathers of the pueo is probably the only one of its kind in existence. Pueo was one of the most venerated of the 'aumakua forms, second perhaps only to mano, the shark. As such, it would not have been sought after by bird catchers. This cape was a gift from Mr. and Mrs. Alfred Ostheimer. It was purchased from the Bray family and was said to have been worn by the Kahuna nui, Hewahewa, a noted priest of the time of Kamehameha the Great. — Photo by Bob Chinn, courtesy of the Honolulu Academy of Arts

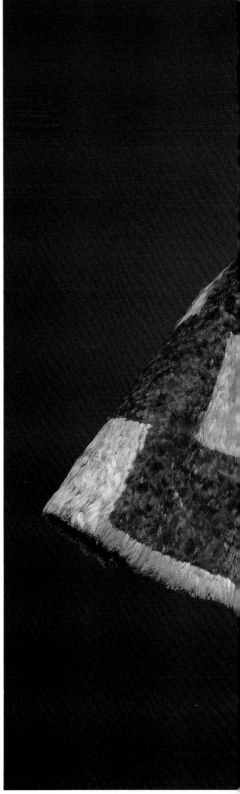

The oblong, or squarish forms seem to be at odds with the usual forms found in feather garments throughout Polynesia. The note of black at the center of the back is startling. Black forms at the front are even more unusual. The placement in relation to the neck and the area of the tie is puzzling—why? There is a purpose to this unique use of black feathers. It makes a point about 'aumakua, 'ohana, or some especially remembered deed. —Photo by Ben Patnoi, courtesy of Bernice Pauahi Bishop Museum

# Notes: The Starbuck Cape

Much has been written about the Starbuck cape. The information in Dr. Brigham's book is current up to his time, but then the cape was acquired after his death by a succeeding director of the Museum and there is a great deal of correspondence in the Museum files concerning this 'ahuli'i. The cape went to Captain Starbuck whose ship carried the King and Queen, Kamehameha II and his wife Kamāmalu, to London in 1824. The captain was very well liked by the royal party and he treated them with great respect and courtesy and made some of the arrangements for their stay in England. Somehow he came into possession of this handsome little cape with its little square-like chunks of yellow. It was probably a gift from Kamehameha II or Boki.

Some of the chunks in the design at the area of the neck appear to be squares, some of them look like oblongs. Squares and oblongs with yellow 'ō'ō feathers solidly placed in a background of red 'i'iwi feathers. There are four irregular shapes around the neck which are made of black 'ō'ō feathers. The sudden touch of black provides the perfect contrasting note. And yet the lack of symmetry in the cape, the unbalanced placement of the black shapes, is an odd note strongly suggesting *kaona* (hidden meanings). The black rectangles may have had a symbolic significance, something religious, or they may even be a record of an event, similar to the practice of naming people by certain happenings. Every mark on objects of ancient Hawai'i was placed there to make a point exceeding a single declaration of the decorative, but since no one bothered to find out the meaning of designs on *'ahu'ula,* today we find it necessary to probe into possible meanings. The great void of information connected with Hawaiian featherwork is as baffling as it is maddening. But, this *'ahu'ula* came back to the museum. It is once again a part of Hawai'i. I'm glad that we have it because it is unusual with the little rectangles.

# Notes: The Kapi'olani Cape

The Kapi'olani cape. I sometimes refer to this cape as the Kapi'olani II cape to distinguish it from the Kapi'olani-nui or Kapi'olani I cape. Kapi'olani II was married to King Kalā-kaua. She was the granddaughter of King Ka-umu-ali'i and, therefore, the great grand-daughter of Kamakahelei of Kaua'i and the high chief of Ka'eo of Maui.

Her cape has a certain striking beauty because of the richer substance of its design. The lines are slender. On a red background, the main crescent of yellow in the center is very thin, stretching almost the width of the cape. It points in between two upside-down sharkfins which give it a certain representational finish. There is a certain predictability in its artistic message. Between the two pairs of fins, and then falling down to the middle back and dipping into the long yellow crescent, is a line of black feathers, the middle of which, at the bottom, looks duodenal. There is a little roundness there, a little swelling, whereas the rest of it is thin and uniform up to the shoulders. From behind, hanging up and not worn, it looks like a lavaliere or a rather handsome necklace on the bodice of a very large woman.

I was struck by this unusual form which I have not seen in any other *'ahu'ula*. It must be a highly individualistic statement concerning the person for which it was made. There is no written history of this garment, no formal *mo'olelo* of which I am aware concerning its origin and its history. Because of the lavaliere black line and its swelling in the middle it is a totally unique specimen of Hawaiian featherwork art.

*There is no written history or formal moʻolelo on the Kapiʻolani cape. The lavaliere black line and its swelling in the middle is unique to Hawaiian featherwork art. — Photo by Ben Patnoi, courtesy of Bernice Pauahi Bishop Museum*

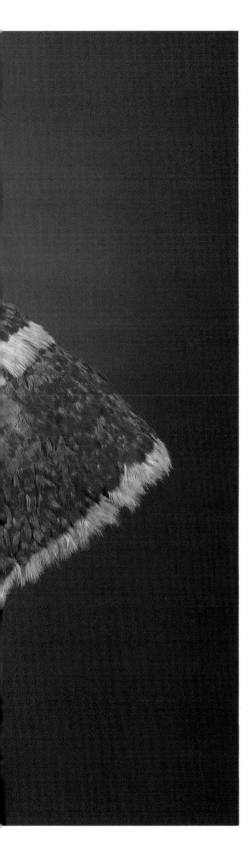

This 'ahuli'i was purchased in London for $600.00 by Queen Kapi'olani during her participation in the Diamond Jubilee of Queen Victoria. In the diary of Queen Kapi'olani, Prince Jonah Kuhio added this note: "One red 'ahu'ula presented by Lot, Kamehameha V in 1857 to E. Faulkner, paymaster of the H.B.M. ship Havannah (sic) and bought by Kapi'olani for $600.00 and returned to Hawai'i." (Brigham Vol 7 #1 pp. 49–50.) Queen Kapi'olani named the 'ahuli'i the "Kekaulike Cape," most likely in honor of her sister Kinoiki Kekaulike, who died unexpectedly in 1883. Princess Kekaulike was a beloved island figure. Many songs were written in her honor. —Photo by Ben Patnoi, courtesy of the Bernice Pauahi Bishop Museum

# Notes: The Kekaulike Cape

The Kekaulike *'ahu'ula* is beguilingly simple in its design. It is mostly red. Two very sharply pointed fin-like projections shoot out from the middle front of the cape, around the chest and to the back. They might be representative of wings of a bird because, wrapped around a person, they give the impression of wings protecting a person. This theme of wings is something new to me, something that I have just latched onto in my discussion of capes and which intrigues me. I think it is a valid possibility to pursue, especially since the bird, the *Ka'iwa 'ālai maka,* the frigate bird, had such an important role in the mythology and poetry of the old culture as a symbol of great powers. These two wings or fin-like forms are certainly *'aumakua* forms. The shark, or the bird, would be protective. The points in the curve that make up what appears to be wings, fin, or talon are of yellow feathers. The rest of the cape is red except for the yellow border at the bottom. The border of the neck is made up of the usual red, black and yellow squares. There are six little fins which come down the middle of the front of the cape. One black in the middle and two yellow on what would be the left side of the cape, two black and one yellow on the right side of the cape, looking at it from the back. It is a handsome cape, complex enough though to be more than a decorative, pleasure garment. I think it has more importance than that.

King Kekaulike of Maui was of the sacred *pi'o* birth. He married his sister, Ke-Ku'i-'apo-'iwa I, and produced three children who became the progenitors of Hawai'i's leading *ali'i* in the early 19th Century. Kalola, the oldest daughter, married Kalani-'ōpu'u of Hawai'i and bore his heir, Kiwala'ō, whom we have mentioned elsewhere. She lived with Keoua and had a daughter, Keku'i'apo'iwa Liliha, who married her half-brother Kiwala'ō and produced in that union Kamehameha's second wife, Ke-'ōpuo-lani. Kamehameha *nui* married his half-sister, Kūkamano, and became ultimately the grandfather of the great Pākī, father of Bernice Pauahi Bishop. With his wife, Ha'alo'u, Kekaulike became the grandfather of Queen Ka'ahumanu, John Kīna'u, Kalanimoku and Boki and his wife Kuini Liliha. Kekaulike was ancestor to all the major chiefs of Hawai'i during the 19th

Century. He was also the father of the ferocious Kahekili, who was tattooed in a checkered pattern down one half of his body and who wore sticks of bamboo to hold open his eyelids during a war in order to look fiercer. Kekaulike was the father of the famous twins Kameʻeiamoku and Kamanawa, who both helped to raise the young Kamehameha in Pololū Valley in the Kohala district. Kamanawa became the grandfather of the Kalākaua's. Kameʻeiamoku was the father of Hoapili-Kāne who married Kaʻahumanu's sister, Kalakua. She had at one time also been one of Kamehameha's wives. Hoapili became the adoptive or *hānai* father of Lot Kapu-a-īwa, Kamehameha V. Lot owned the beautiful Kekaulike cape which came back to Hawaiʻi from England when it was purchased by Queen Kapiʻolani, also a descendant of Kekaulike by way of his son Kaʻeo who was the great grandfather of Queen Kapiʻolani.

Kekaulike produced many heirs, among them the most important chiefs in Hawaiʻi during the era of Kamehameha and the decades that followed. The Kalākaua family arched back to Kekaulike through Queen Kapiʻolani, Kameʻeiamoku and Kamanawa and two grandfathers and a great uncle of the Kalakauas.

Princess Kinoʻiki Kekaulike was one of two sisters of Queen Kapiʻolani. Princess Kekaulike and her sister, Princess Poʻomaikelani, lived at Hale ʻAimoku on lower Punchbowl Street next to my great grandparents, Owen and Hanakaulani Holt, in the neighborhood called both Honuakaha and Apua. There was always talk in the family about how beautiful Kekaulike was and how she was always the life of the party, gifted as a chantress and highly skilled as a *hula* dancer.

Aunty Jenny Wilson, who grew up in the same neighborhood, remembered Kinoʻike Kekaulike well. She said Princess Kekaulike was extremely popular among native Hawaiians and had a large following of admirers who came frequently to Hale ʻAimoku to serenade the princess and to perform versions of *hula* danced from *mele* which she had composed. "In my day," Aunty Jenny Wilson said, "Kekaulike was the most beloved *aliʻi* of them all."

*This little cape is said to have been worn by Princess Pauahi (Mrs. Charles R. Bishop) as a child and a young girl when she attended the Kula Keiki Ali'i. It emphatically divides into two parts, the design forms and the feathers, as if to make the statement of an equal division of some kind relating to Pauahi personally. The cape was probably designed and made for her in the 1830s. The tooth and/or fin forms are sharply difinitive, almost exact in each instance. The black and red divisions at the back of the cape are not so exact in the division of the two colors. They may suggest Pele and the stopping of her fires. The black becomes cooled lava. — Photo by Ben Patnoi, courtesy of Bernice Pauahi Bishop Museum*

146

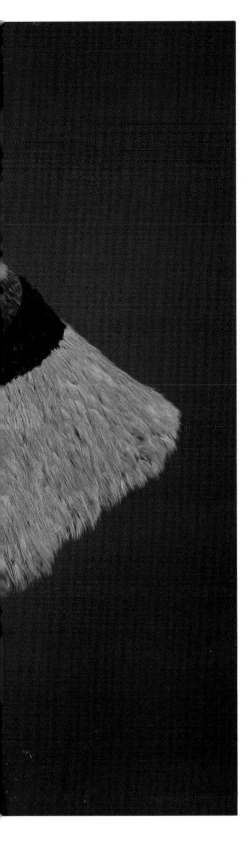

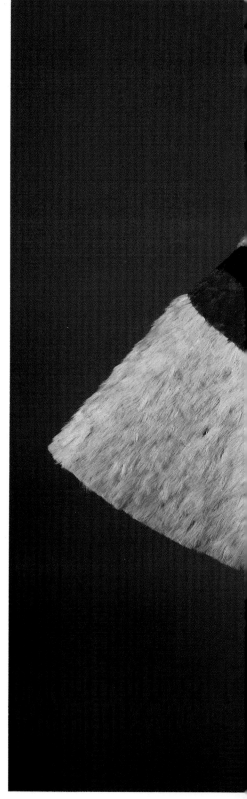

In the front view, the boldness of the design is strengthened by the bottom pair of fin-like forms. This is achieved with black feathers fixed in one-and-a-half inch bands. The motif is repeated with red feathers in the area of the wearer's neck. Pointed crescent ends of black and red feathers swoop into the design between the red and black forms. In the rear view, the two parallel bands that begin opened ended in the front become joined at the rear as opposite red crescents. Below this are heavy curving bands of red and black feathers. — Photo by Ben Patnoi, courtesy of Bernice Pauahi Bishop Museum

149

# Notes: The Franklin Cape

This cape has become known as the "Franklin Cape," because it was given to Lady Jane Franklin, widow of Sir John Franklin, by Kamehameha IV and his consort, Queen Emma, in 1861. Lady Franklin visited Hawai'i in that year, taking respite from the arduous traveling she had undertaken in search of her husband, a famed explorer of his time who had disappeared with his ship and his crew during exploration of the southern tip of the southern hemisphere. He had sailed extensively in the Pacific, ranging from Alaska to Australia before penetrating the rather unknown and forbidding regions of Antarctica. Kamehameha IV was intrigued with Lady Franklin—as an *ali'i* from a foreign place and as the first *haole* woman *ali'i* to come to Hawai'i. And she was intrigued with the King because he was the first Polynesian monarch she had ever met. They became great friends. They took to each other and spent much time admiring and appreciating each other's gifts. Lady Franklin wrote in her journal with surprise and delight at how well the King spoke English, and she was happy to note that he spoke it with an English accent.

The King was taken with Lady Franklin's manners, her good mind and her aristocratic behavior generally. She became genuinely interested in Hawai'i and spent much time with the King and others during her visit, learning specific details about the royal family, gathering facts as well as gossip about Hawai'i generally, and showing an attitude of good will toward Hawai'i and its people. When Queen Emma visited England in 1865 to raise money for the Anglican Mission in Hawai'i, Lady Franklin generously offered her services to help the Queen pursue her goal. She housed the Hawaiian Queen and her party for a number of weeks in her home, Upper Gore Lodge, near London. The British government, in time, installed Queen Emma in Claridge's Hotel. Lady Franklin kept a journal during some of the time she spent in Hawai'i, but her niece Sophia Cracroft, wrote long, journal-style letters home to England, describing what was happening during their visit to Hawai'i. Miss Cracroft describes the ceremony in which this cape, which has come to be known as the Lady Franklin cape, was given to her aunt by Kamehameha IV. (See Alfons Korn, The Victorian Visitors, p. 157)

The feathers in the Lady Franklin cape are brilliant in color. They look as though they had been plucked from live birds only a few days before. The cape has several crescents in its design. In fact, it is built up on crescents. It also has a predominantly yellow background. I'd say that 85 percent of the area of the cape is of yellow feathers—from the *mamo* and *'ō'ō.* There are the two fin-like projections that begin at the shoulders. Those are made of black and red feathers. Inside those, around the neck, are two distinct crescents—very sharply pointed, and those are made of red feathers. These are just sort of wide lines with yellow in the center. The red feathers create the border of the crescents as the black feathers constitute the border of the black fins below. Around the neck, in the usual fashion of arrangement, the small red, yellow then black and yellow squares create a softness of the neck when worn without other garments. It was a comfort to have this softness instead of the relative roughness of the *'olonā* fibers of a net backing. Then in the middle of the cape, which would have made it the most strongly visible element in the design from the back, are two crescents or a half moon. The one half crescent is of black feathers and the other, joining it below with nothing in between, is a large crescent with red feathers. Here again you see the profound abstractions of this design, haughtily non-representational elements—forms that suggest nothing but vague moons and vague fins. They are so abstract that they are pure spirit. They're formless, unrelated in a slavish way to forms and shapes in nature. You must work your eyes and your spirit and your intelligence to an exhausting degree to draw from this design its meaning in terms of *'aumakua* (family guardians), *'ohana* (family or clan) and the person's relationship to the timeless stretches of the universe. I used to look at the Lady Franklin cape and think, "Oh, my God, what an ordinary design. What a tiresome, tiresome design." Yet, I know, feeling through it, looking at it as a Hawaiian who grew up with chiefly mores, and told about the feathers, told about what they are, and told about their great value as spiritual things, that they had to be respected, certainly had to be cared for, if you have them around. I have quite a different feeling when I look at this garment now. The Lady Franklin cape has been returned to Hawai'i through the generosity of her descendants—her *'ohana,* the Austens and the Le Froys. It is now in the collection of the Bernice Pauahi Bishop Museum.

The elaborate design at the front of the Kapena Cape suggests 'aumakua from one of the families of crustacea. In the Kumulipo, man is linked to creatures of the sea, and these in turn are paired with life forms on land: insects, plants, mammals (Johnson, Rubellite, the Kumulipo, Vol. I). 'Aumakua implies continuum and relationship, the enduring integuments of life.
—Photo by Ben Patnoi, courtesy of Bernice Pauahi Bishop Museum

# Notes: The Kapena Cape

[1] Hawaiian Featherwork, Vol. 1, p. 79

William T. Brigham wrote in some detail about the Kapena Cape. "This Cape is made of *'ō'ō* feathers with *'i'iwi* and black *'ō'ō*. The net is in three pieces and of good quality."[1] This *'ahuli'i* is tiny—one of the smallest I have seen. It appears to have been made for a child.

This garment belonged to John Kapena's daughter, Leihulu, and was in her possession when Doctor Brigham wrote about the Kapena Cape. Leihulu had no heirs and it is now, I can happily say, in the Bishop Museum collection. Leihulu Kapena was also known as Alexandra. She was Honolulu's leading pageant director in her time. She was recognized as a fine pianist who taught and studied music at Saint Andrew's Priory. She was a very close friend of my great aunt, the composer Eliza Holt. I heard a lot about the Kapenas from my parents. They lived in a large wooden house which sat under several monkey pod trees on Kamehameha IV Road in Kalihi. John Kapena was from a Hawai'i family of chiefs, but he spent most of his life in Honolulu serving the Hawaiian government in one capacity or another. During the period he spent as King Kalākaua's Minister of Finance, he journeyed with the King to Washington to petition for a Treaty of Reciprocity with the United States. The King and his commission were successful in bringing this about in 1875.

The Kapena Cape has a very large crescent across the middle of the back, very large indeed, and a quite unusual finish and design around the neck. There are red half-circles that lead up the front of the chest toward the neck, and in the middle of the red of the half-circles are little fin-like areas of black, edged with yellow. From the front the back fins become eyes. There are yellow fins cutting into the red half-circles and red fins below. There is a fine balance of yellow *'ō'ō* and red *'i'iwi* in this cape. Seen from the back, there is a little tiny black crescent which is part of a very large yellow crescent, under which there is the large red crescent. Then the rest of the cape is made of yellow feathers. It certainly suggests a cape of importance and one that is not purely decorative. There's enough mystery in this tiny *'ahuli'i* to give a mystifying appearance to its design. It is not an obvious work of art, balancing forms on the right and left sides of the garment in a neat geometric way. For instance, looking at the cape hanging, one gets the feeling that the black in the little red crescents are eyes and the black at the bottom of the red crescents would be a mouth, and the yellow on the black is an even larger mouth, and the red is an even larger mouth still; but they are not mouths. The black and the yellow and the red are symbols of birds—again, protective birds wrapping themselves around the wearer. But there is always balance in these designs. They're not so free-form that they are not balanced off from one side to the next, from the back to the front. It is in the area between the forms that create the design, the areas around the applique of the design, that these things are lifted to the realm of art.

Somehow, just the studied use of the expanse of yellow or red as a background is vitally important to both the esthetic result and the social and spiritual implications of the complete garment. It has been said that color in itself made reference to the island from which a chief originated. That yellow, for example, had to do with one's ancestral connection to the Island of 'O'ahu, and red and black were colors connected with the Island of Hawai'i, and a descent from Pele. The combinations of red, black and yellow and to what extent each color was used were also connected to the islands of Kaua'i, Maui and Moloka'i. Blood of the greatest chiefs of all the islands was mixed in the ruling families of each island. Such a blending of high ranking families in one's ancestry could be boldly registered in the way colors were used. We see in some capes and cloaks a balanced mixture of red and yellow implying strong connections to Maui and 'O'ahu perhaps—and a minimal use of black. Always in these unique garments the use of color combines both the artistic and the practical. Gods, family connections and place of origin—simple facts pertaining to an individual—are stunningly captured in abstract designs implanted in a mass of red or yellow. The result becomes an esthetic *tour de force*. These masses of background are very important to the fact of design, to the impressions. Since the capes and cloaks had to be seen, since they did represent ancestors, gods, *'aumakua*, one must feel one's way through a labyrinth of possibilities seen in color, form and design in order to understand why a particular chief wore a particular garment.

Creatures from the ocean, creatures from the air, creatures from land—all were incorporated into these designs that lean so heavily on the form of the crescent, the tips of the crescents, fin-like shapes or, for that matter, geometric forms such as circles, triangles or the diamond. Without these forms which illustrated the link between family gods, *'ohana* relationships and perhaps more personal details pertaining to a person's life, we would not easily understand why these garments would have been used at all in such a warm place as Hawai'i. In looking carefully at capes and cloaks we see that more attention was paid to the front of capes than of cloaks. We can clearly see this in the Kapena *'ahuli'i* where the design of the front is very carefully worked out as compared to the less carefully worked out cloaks where there is greater looseness over the stomach and loins. The cloaks were of such a length that this dictated the ultimate artistic statement and, whether you have fins or teeth or tail ends of feathers, this was determined by the garment and its function. It is quite possible that you have forms resembling tips of feathers at the front of a cape, because, when the cape is secured at the neck, the front is more or less closed. These little ends of crescents then meet in the middle and they create another bird or another protective encompassing form. In the William Dampier portrait of Princess Nāhi'ena'ena[2] this is very much apparent.

[2] Painted 1825 by William Dampier, Honolulu Academy of Arts collection.

*155*

The emphatic symmetry, the bold shapes composed of red and black feathers, produce an effect that is less imaginative than it is open and bold, like a military command. Yellow 'ō'ō areas provide a strong foundation in which to imbed the distinct red and yellow forms. All is balanced, poised. There is tension and serenity in the cape. We are reminded that in the 1820s and 1830s, Kapi'olani-nui was a chiefess of high rank and authority. —Photo by Ben Patnoi, courtesy of Bernice Pauahi Bishop Museum

# Notes: The Kapiʻolani-nui Cape

The Kapiʻolani-nui cape is an outstanding example of Hawaiian feather art. It has a predominately yellow background and it uses red and black feathers in equal quantities for the execution of symbols. It is the balance of the coloration that is so striking. The black and the red are fused in the center crescent, which encircles the neck. These crescents are long, thin, more wing-like than fin-like. Below the chest is another fusion of red and black, the forms being more fin-like than wing-like. They sit in a mass of yellow and the whole creates an effect of rigorous balance. The yellow feathers are very beautiful. The pale yellow feathers are a mix of probably ʻōʻō and *mamo,* otherwise this cape would have a strong orange luster. The color schemes are very handsome and the design is well conceived to accommodate the choice of colors used in the creation of this cape. The Kapiʻolani-nui cape has a strong no-nonsense look.

The black feathers in this *ʻahuliʻi* seem to be a statement about Pele—the lineage from Pele. Pele is the *ʻaumakua.* But yellow is the important color with respect to ʻOʻahu. Some chiefs of the greatest rank were born on ʻOʻahu. As a matter of fact, Kū-kani-loko, where the birthing rocks are, is where most high chiefs and chiefesses were born a long, long time ago. They journeyed from all islands for the bearing of children at Kū-kani-loko. Many chiefs of the highest rank, no matter from what island, almost invariably had ʻOʻahu antecedents. The Piʻilani of Maui and the Keawe all had ancestors who were ʻOʻahu chiefs of very high rank. The genealogies of Kamehameha and his cousins are heavily infused with the blood of royal ʻOʻahu chiefs. King Kalākaua and Queen Liliʻuokalani were descended from some of these same individuals. The great Chief ʻIwikauikaua, brother of Kahikilaulani of Puna, came to ʻOʻahu to find a mate of equal rank. The mother of Kalani-ʻōpuu, Kamaka-ʻimoku, was brought up in Kaʻu but she was the daughter of an ʻOʻahu chief, Kū-a-nuʻuanu. Kalani-nui-ʻī-a-mamao, Kalani-ʻōpuu's father was the grandson of the famous chiefess of ʻOʻahu, Keakealani, the highest ranking Hawaiian of her era. Their first child, Keakealani, became the ancestress of most Hawaiian chiefs, from the late 17th Century on. Kamakahelei, hereditary high chiefess of Kauaʻi, took the ʻOʻahu *piʻo* chief, Kaneoneo, as her husband, but, unfortunately, there were no children from this union.

*The chief Ha'alele'a who was married to the Princess Ke-kau'ōnohi. She left him a number of priceless feather objects which are now in the collection of the Honolulu Academy of Arts. (See page 165 for further details.) – Courtesy of the Hawaii State Archives.*

# Appendices

## Feather Girdles: Tahitian Origins

In Tahiti, the royal feather girdles of Polynesia seemed to have their greatest importance as social-political objects denoting a family or families having the highest claim to the highest office. The *maro ura*, the girdle, made of sennit and feathers, usually functioned in close connection with a family *marae* (temple) as one of the symbols of undisputed power and control. There were two families with ancient claim to the possession of feather girdles in Tahiti, the chiefs of Vaiari and the chiefs of Puna'auia. The Vaiari chief ruled over the Teva people, the preeminent clan of Tahiti. The *maro ura* of the Tevas had ancient status and perhaps, as feathers go, it was imbued with the greatest degree of *mana* as an object symbolizing power. The Teva *maro ura* was named Te-Ra'i-Pua-Tata. The *maro ura* of the Puna'auia was probably as ancient and powerful as a symbol, and the formal title of this family was Tetua-nui-e-marua-e-te-Ra'i.

The *maro ura* were invented and worn to glorify power of birth and to exhibit status; they hung loose over brown bodies during investiture and their red and yellow feathers glimmered bright in the sun, singing the praises of the age old glory of the great clans. The *maro ura* of Tahiti, as in Hawai'i, were about ten feet long and constructed of *'olonā* matting and feathers. At their ends there were rows of teeth taken from high chiefs and fish. Various symbolization of mysterious family signs were incorporated in oblong areas along the sash in the Tahitian girdles, but, for the most part, the Hawaiian girdle, or sash, is almost totally free of abstract symbols. *'Ō'ō* feathers edge the entire girdle, thereby framing the center oblong of red *'i'iwi* feathers.

The Vaiari *maro* and that of the Puna'auia were undisputed garments of power until late in the 18th Century when the Pomare clan with the help of the British began to establish themselves as the ruling family of Tahiti. The creation of their *maro ura* is a strange but wonderfully Polynesian story. Captain Samuel Wallis of HMS *The Dolphin* anchored in Matavai Bay in 1767 and ordered the English naval pennant raised in preparation of the formal assumption of British protection of Tahiti. Tahitians approached the pennant and—instead of paying it the respect expected by the British—they first presented ordinary plantain branches as an act of homage. They then pelted the pennant with stones—a bewildering act of defiance to the British. Finally, the tattered pennant was carried off to the Marae Mahaiatea where the high chiefs Amo and Purea were to make and store a *maro ura* for their son Terii'irere. It was a brilliant coup on the part of his parents to build this closeness to the English, especially while the Vaiari and Puna'auia high chiefs were absent from the area. Some historians say that this act settled family disputes in the Papara region (see Henry Adams, *Memories of Arii Taimai E*) and greatly helped them to establish *maro ura* rights.

Amo and Purea had legitimate reasons for wanting to establish the *maro ura* (which became "cynically" known as the "Wallis *maro ura*"). They were *ali'i* of some rank in the Matavai area and were in command of a *marae* in a corner of Papara. But, upon learning of the Amo-Purea and Captain Wallis' intentions, a fierce battle developed when Tevas and their cousins returned to Matavai. The struggle was ended fairly quickly and won by the Tevas, and then the Wallis *maro* and its war god or *oro* were placed in the ancestral temple of Amo and Purea and somehow fell into the hands of Tu who became Pomare I. Henry Adams and the Teva-Salmons claim "he seized it."

A new girdle was manufactured, a new god

attached to it, and these became the *maro ura* and *oro* of Tu and his clan, the Pomares. Undoubtedly they (the Pomares) had established themselves with Captain Wallis—as closely as Amo and Purea. The Teva and their cousins were away from Matavai much of the time in those days that Captain Wallis was there and so were never acknowledged by him as the pre-eminent tribe of Tahiti. He was therefore naively and subjectively influenced at first by Purea and Amo and later by Tu.

After this there is no doubt but that the Pomare clan had established its rule and power over the people of Tahiti, although their *maro ura* establishes them as *arii nouveau* and not up to the high rank of the ancient regime of chiefs. The Pomare usurped the mighty Teva as high chiefs. They became equipped with temple, *oro* and newly manufactured *maro ura* when opportunity arose and became, with the help of Captain Wallis (whose uncertain and naive notions of native social organization of an ancient society upset the chief) rulers of Tahiti in perpetuity. The Pomares even married, in time, into the ancient Teva clan. Henry Adams has written about this in an unusual work of genealogy and history privately published in Paris.

One of the main sources of my information concerning the royal feather girdles of Tahiti comes from a splendid paper, *Symbols of Sovereignty, Feather Girdles of Tahiti and Hawai'i,* Department of Anthropology Bernice Pauahi Bishop Museum, Honolulu, Hawai'i, written by Roger Rose. The other source I found most useful, and at times quite amusing, was an interesting Henry Adams publication which I discovered one day at the New York Public Library. The private copy from which I worked had once belonged to Adam's brother, the historian Brooks Adams. It was copy number three of ten copies privately printed in Paris.

Adams paid a long visit to the Tati Salmon family in Papapora in 1891. (Tati Salmon was the eldest son of Alexander Salmon, a London Jew who settled before 1838 in Tahiti, and the chiefess Arii Taimai E Arii Nui O Tahiti. They were also the parents of Queen Marae, married at one time to Pomare IV). During that visit he worked with the old Salmon chiefess, the ranking Teva of her time known as Arii Taimai E Arii Nui O Tahiti.

In this remarkable enclave of high chiefs both Teva and Pomare strains were present at the rambling old house of Jaques Tati Salmon. For as long as Adams was in Tahiti, the Papara group sat day and night and, with the great old chiefess' extraordinary help, they put together the story of the loss of Teva power—the girdle and *oro* and their place in the temple of the Tevas. It made for a remarkable story that has come together very well for me with the help of Roger Rose's papers. Lengthy genealogical charts were designed for Adam's use and much ancient history of the family is offered in his work—a masterpiece of history and genealogy.

*This Hawaiian feather piece is known as Liloa's girdle and is part of the Bernice Pauahi Bishop Museum Collection. —Courtesy of the Bernice Pauahi Bishop Museum*

# Hawaiian Feather Girdles

Very little is known about Hawaiian feather girdles—who made them, who used them and for what reason. Queen Lili'uokalani had kept a sacred *malo* under her bed for safe keeping. During the frequent trips she made away from Hawai'i, Colonel 'Iaukea, her steward, took to placing this priceless garment in a vault at Bishop Bank, then returning it to its home under the Queen's bed at Washington Place only when it became known that she was returning.

There is a single splendid specimen of an intact *malo* in the collection of the Bernice Pauahi Bishop Museum. It is called the feather *malo* of Līloa—who apparently kept it at his home in Waipi'o Valley. It went to his son 'Umi—a figure well known in Hawaiian lore—and after that it fell into obscurity and was not known to have existed until its discovery by King Kalākaua. It was inherited by his sister, Queen Lili'uokalani, who, at the urging of some of the leading *ali'i*, later gave it into the care of the Bishop Museum. The defeathered remnant of another *malo* is also in the museum's collection.

There is one piece of lore which has come down from the time of Queen Keakealani which clearly establishes the institutional concerns of her use of a feather girdle and its importance in declaring the *kapu* status of young chiefs by the highest ruling figures of their time. In this episode, Queen Keakealani commanded authority to invest use of the girdle of Līloa upon her grandson Ka-'Ī-amamao, son of the high chief Keaweikekahi. The incident of this investiture recalls somewhat the Tahitian traditional draping of a feather *malo* over a young chief destined to rule. Keaweikekahi's womb sister, Kalanikauleleia'iwi, lived with her brother (in Hawai'i's chiefly style of sibling

marriage) and produced a son, Kalaninui'e'e'aumoku, known better to us as Ke'eaumoku, the father of Queen Ka'ahumanu. Earlier, Ke'eaumoku's grandmother had draped a famed feather girdle of Līloa over the eldest child of Keawe, the young chief Ka-'Ī-amamao. Kalanikauleleia'iwi was infuriated by this act, which she considered a usurpation of her and her son's rank (her child was a Ni'aupi'o, brother/sister product as compared to the rank of her brother's son, Ka-'Ī-amamao whose mother was beneath Kalanikauleleia'iwi). This is all told to us by Roger Rose in his *Symbols of Sovereignty Feather Girdles of Tahiti and Hawai'i*. This piece of intriguing and historically valuable information (the investiture of Keakealani's grandsons) was discovered in Hale Nauwā or Board of Genealogy papers (1886-8-11). There was a great discussion between mother and daughter about rank and the right to investiture. Rank was of such importance to the high chiefs that some of them murdered to win advantage, committed suicide from embarassment over someone, or even placed themselves in voluntary exile over an issue of rank of importance that involved ignoring of a *kapu*. When children were deliberately allowed to climb over the sacred ones, for example, it was an act considered so extremely demeaning that suicide or exile was a lower ranking person's only recourse.

There were also degrees of veneration connected with rank: the *kapu moe* (prostration), the *kapu wela* (burning fire) and the *kapu wohi* among others. These were the *kapu* reserved for the highest ranking chiefs. The *moe* and *wela kapu* were reserved for sacred chiefs of full brother-sister parentage. *Wohi* was reserved for *niau pi'o* chiefs, the offspring of half-brother/half-sister marriages—as in the case of Kalanikauleleia'iwi and her brother Keawe. Keawe had extracted from his mother, the great Chiefess Keakealani, the *kapu moe* and *kapu wela* for his son Ka-'Ī-amamao, although this child was not the result of a union with a full sister. Kalanikauleleia'iwi's child Ke'eaumoku was of the same rank as his father, as was the high chief Keawe a half-brother to Kalanikauleleia'iwi.

The two boys were rivals for being granted the highest *kapu,* even though Keawe obviously preceeded his sister Kalanikauleleia'iwi. As a result of the confrontation between mother and daughter over the investiture of Ka-'Ī-amamao and Ke'eaumoku, Keakealani (according to the Board of Genealogy records cited above) took the girdle from its calabash repository and draped Ke'eaumoku in the same way as she had her other grandson. As she draped him she established for him and his descendants the *kapu wohi* which has come down to his descendants to this very day. The *kapu wohi* allows those who possess it to stand in the presence of *ali'i* who are of *kapu moe* rank. It also allows a *wohi* to stand aside politely but without physical show of veneration for those who possess the *kapu wela* or the *kapu moe.*

Royal feather girdles seemed to have a deeper, stronger position in use governing rank and rulership in Tahiti. It could be that in Hawai'i the use of so many other garments of royal and noble significance usurped the importance of feather girdles. The great cloaks with their elaborate symbolic designs, the capes with their designs, the awesome *kāhili,* the helmets and the *lei* may have come to supercede in importance something as simple and as limited an object of adornment as a feather girdle. Nowhere in the notation of the first known foreign visitors from Europe is there mention of a feather girdle, though their writings sparkle with references to those pieces of Hawaiian featherwork art which have to us the most important link to rank and power.

## Little Feather Houses and Little Feather Mats

Little feather houses and mats were made by the Hawaiians, but almost nothing is known about these intriguing examples. They were collected, carried off to Europe, and the best example of a house now reposes in Vienna's Völkerkunde Museum. Their shape would suggest that they might have stored tiny household gods. They suggest a place where prayers were said, or perhaps they were a special repository for highly venerated creations.

The little mat-like objects, which Dr. Kaeppler refers to as feathered aprons, "likely to have been worn, because they have loops and lacing reminiscent of Hawaiian ankle ornaments" (*Artificial Curiosities,* 1978, p. 59), also remain unexplained. On both of these objects collected by Cook or members of his company, the designs appear to be quite different from those found on the *'ahu'ula.* In fact, they strongly resemble some of the patterns found in Navajo rugs.

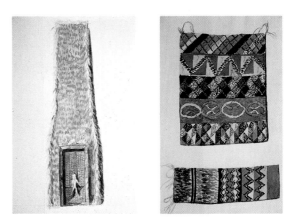

*Nothing has been documented concerning the use of this unique house-like structure nor of the little feather mats next to it. —Courtesy of the Bernice Pauahi Bishop Museum*

## Coney-Ha'alele'a Feather Objects

In honor of the 50th anniversary, December 1976, of the Honolulu Academy of Arts, Mrs. Andrew McKee gave to that institution a handsome gift of Hawaiian featherwork. In the gift there were five splendid feather *lei* and two capes which were in excellent condition, one of unusual design.

Aside from the intrinsic value of this gift—and its meaning to Hawai'i as a composite of Hawaiian featherwork—it represents a treasury of Hawaiian art which remained in one family for several generations. The *'ahu'ula* and *lei* of this group were kept in the Coney family of Kaua'i for almost a hundred years, coming down to this family by way of marriage, the marriage of Amoe Ena to the Chief Ha'alele'a. These Coney-Ha'alele'a feathers originally belonged to the High Chiefess Kekau'ōnohi, a granddaughter of King Kamehameha. She married Levi Ha'alele'a in 1847.

The High Chiefess was the daughter of the High Chief Kaho'ānō-Kū Kīna'u, the son of the High Chiefess Pele'uli and King Kamehameha. Kekau'ōnohi's mother was the High Chiefess Kahakuha'ako'i of the Maui royal family. Kekau'ōnohi was an *ali'i* of considerable influence during the middle 1830s until the time of her death in 1847. In 1858, Amoe Ena (the child of an early Chinese storekeeper and young Hawaiian girl of *ali'i* lineage) was married to the Chief Ha'alele'a, widower of the royal Chiefess Kekau'ōnohi.

Six years after they were married the Chief Ha'alele'a died. Mrs. Ha'alele'a inherited the handsome house abutting the palace compound and facing Washington Place on Beretania Street. It was a two-story structure which had the appearance of some early California dwellings made of stone and mortar. She lived there until her death in 1904. Ena Ha'alele'a inherited the lands and personal property of her chiefly husband. Among these possessions were the splendid *'ahu'li'i* and *lei* which are now a part of the collection of the Honolulu Academy of Arts.

*The first 'ahuli'i in the collection of the Honolulu Academy of Arts has a plain yellow back reminiscent of Kamehameha's mamo 'ahu'ula. The cape is a fine example of understatement in Hawaiian feather art. The finish around the neck has the appearance of a lei hulu. On the front of the cape are four fin or teeth-like forms which appear on the front of many cloaks and capes. They are particularly distinct in this garment and a bold declaration of the protective powers of 'aumakua and 'ohana.—Photo by Bob Chinn, courtesy of the Honolulu Academy of Arts*

*(Following pages) Hearts are an anomaly as an artistic metaphor in Polynesia, suggesting strongly that this 'ahuli'i was made after 1779. The cape belonged to the high chiefess Kekau'ōnohi, who in tongue-and-cheek style may have been trying to immortalize her husband, Levi Ha'alele'a, a handsome man known to be immensely popular with the ladies. —Photo by Bob Chinn, courtesy of the Honolulu Academy of Arts*

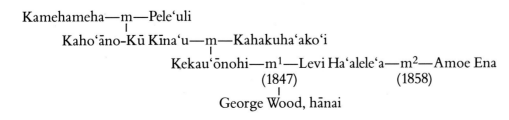

These double Coney-Haʻaleleʻa leis are in excellent condition. The green ʻōʻū feathers are bright, almost luminescent, with yellow mamo and ʻōʻō feathers in vibrant contrast to the green. There are both koʻo mamo and ēʻē feathers of the ʻōʻō in these leis, which give them a marvelous texture. Koʻo tends to have a sturdy compact look in the finished article, while the ʻēʻē feathers of the ʻōʻō have a light, fluffy appearance. Even in color there is a difference. ʻŌʻō feathers are pale yellow, the color of lemons. Mamo feathers are golden yellow, almost orange. When the two feathers are combined in a lei, the result is quite handsome. The ʻēʻē feathers give it the appearance of weightlessness—splashes of pale yellow sprouting from the more compact koʻo mamo feathers. — Photo by Bob Chinn, courtesy of the Honolulu Academy of Arts

# Glossary

**A**

| | |
|---|---|
| *'ahuli'i* | feather cape |
| *'ahu'ula* | feather cloak |
| *'akialoa* | honeycreepers with long curved bill |
| *Akua hulu manu* | feather gods |
| *ali'i* | chief, chiefess, King, Queen, noble, royal |
| *'ape'ape* | huge leafed forest perennial herb with thick prostrate stem rising at the tip to about four feet |
| *'aumakua* | Family or personal god(s) |

**E**

| | |
|---|---|
| *'ē'ē* | yellow underwing feathers of the *'ō'ō* |
| *'eu'eu* | exciting, rousing, alert, lively, animated, aroused |

**H**

| | |
|---|---|
| Hawai'i | both the island and the group of islands |
| Hi'i-aka | name of the twelve younger sisters of the goddess Pele |
| *hula* | dance, both sacred and entertaining |

**I**

| | |
|---|---|
| *'i'iwi* | scarlet Hawaiian honeycreeper found on all the main islands; main source of red feathers for Hawaiian art. |
| *'io* | Hawaiian Hawk, a god |

**K**

| | |
|---|---|
| Ka'eo | chief of Ka'ū and Kona, Kalani-'ōpu'u's son, full, as food calabash, full of knowledge, strong, zealous |
| *kāhili* | feather standard, symbolic of royalty |
| *kāhili lele* | smaller *kāhili* referred to also as a fly wisk |
| *kahu* | honored attendant, guardian, nurse, keeper, pastor of a church |
| Kākuhihewa | great chief of 'O'ahu, ancestor of 'O'ahu rulers through Kamahana |
| *kalae'iwa* | frigate or man-of-war bird, also *Ka 'iwa 'ālai maka* |
| Kalani-'ōpu'u | the great high chief who ruled Hawai'i in Kamehameha's youth |
| Kama-pua'a | name of a pig god famous in legends; he frequently taunted Pele |
| Kamehameha | the great Pai'ea, a chief of distinction and greatness |
| *kāmoe* | to go straight ahead, to recline, flatten, *kāmoe* style *lei* |
| Kanaloa | name of one of the great Hawaiian gods, called a god of healing |
| *kāne* | male, husband, man |
| Kaneoneo | a *pi'o* born chief of 'O'ahu—grandson of Peleioholani, married for a time to Kamakahelei. |
| *kānoa* | bowl, as for kava; hollow of land, pit, circular |
| *kapa* | formerly clothes of any kind, or bed clothes |
| *kapu* | taboo, prohibition, sacredness, forbidden |
| *kapu moe* | prostration taboo |
| Kaua'i | one of the major islands in the Hawaiian Islands chain |
| *kauila /kauwila* | a native tree in the buckthorn family |
| *koa* | the largest of native forest trees with light gray bark |
| *koa'e* | tropical or boatswain bird |

| | |
|---|---|
| *ko'o mamo* | the larger yellow feathers of the *mamo* |
| Kū | one of the four major gods |
| *kū'auhau* | genealogy, pedigree, genealogist, historian |
| Kūka'ilimoku | family god given Kamehameha by Kalani-'ōpu'u; thereafter called war god. |
| Kumuhana | son of Peleioholani and the last hereditary high chief of 'O'ahu |
| *kūpuna* | grandparents, ancestors |

**L**

| | |
|---|---|
| *lei* | garland, wreath, necklace of flowers or feathers |
| *lei hulu* | feather *lei* |
| *lei pāni'o* | *lei* with spiral design |
| Lohi'au | prince of Kaua'i; a tragic and unsuccessful suitor of Pele and Hi'i-aka; especially vulnerable to Pele's wiles |
| Lono | one of the four major gods brought from Tahiti |

**M**

| | |
|---|---|
| *mahiole* | feather helmets |
| *mai nei loko* | from the inside, from the gut level |
| *malo* | male loincloth, also royal specimens made of feathers |
| *mamo* | black Hawaiian honeycreeper, yellow feathers above and below the tail were used in choice feather work |
| *mana* | supernatural or divine power |
| *moa* | chicken, wild chicken—some of its feathers were used in making capes and helmets for chiefs of lesser rank. |

**N**

| | |
|---|---|
| *naupaka* | native species of shrubs found in mountains and along beaches. Hereditary home of sea birds whose feathers were used for the making of *kahili*. |
| Nihoa Island | island between Kaua'i and Midway |
| *niho manō* | shark tooth design |
| *niho palaoa* | whale tooth, whale-tooth pendant, a symbol of royalty of braided human hair and carved whale tooth |
| Ni'ihau | name of one of the Hawaiian Islands |

**O**

| | |
|---|---|
| 'O'ahu | name of one of the major islands in the Hawaiian chain |
| 'ohana | family, relative, kin group, related |
| 'ōhi'a-lehua | a tree with many forms, from tall trees to low shrubs; leaves round and narrow and blunt or pointed and smooth or woolly; the flowers are red, rarely salmon, pink, yellow and white |
| 'olonā fibers | a native shrub |
| 'ō'ō | a black honey-eater with yellow feathers in a tuft under each wing, which were used for featherwork |
| 'ō'ū | a finch like Hawaiian creeper with an almost parrot like bill; its green feathers were used in making cloaks and lei |

**P**

| | |
|---|---|
| Pākini Heiau | ancient temple in Kahuku region of Ka'ū; it is located high above the sea on the lower slopes of Mauna Loa. |
| Pele | name of the volcano goddess, the great earth maker of ancient times; still venerated by some Hawaiians |
| *pani'o* | smooth |
| *paukū* | to make a *lei* with sections of different colors |
| Peleioholani | *pi'o* high chief of 'O'ahu |
| Pi'ilani of Maui | ruling family of Maui |
| *pi'o* | children resulting from sibling matings |

**Q**

| | |
|---|---|
| Queen Kamakahelei | hereditary high chiefess or queen of Kaua'i and Niihau |

**W**

| | |
|---|---|
| Waimea Bay | on 'O'ahu a spectacular surfing place on the North Shore; on Kaua'i a bay and place at the southwest side of the island; where Captain Cook and company stopped for a few days during the first visit |

**U**

| | |
|---|---|
| *'ulī'ulī* | gourd rattle, containing seeds with colored feathers at the top, used for *hula* |

## Note on Orthography of Hawaiian

The orthographic use of macrons and glottals has been determined in accordance with the latest edition of the Puku'i-Elbert *Hawaiian Dictionary* (1971), with the exception of the use of the dash in names of Hawaiian *ali'i*. The reader will find that the use of the dash is one of convenience and not of linguistic principle in separating neophological particles and determiners from bases and modifiers. Some names are left as they have been spelled in traditional literature, and some contain dashes merely to authenticate or to reveal the suggested meanings. More scholarship will be needed before we presume to "establish" the correctly identified meanings of the *ali'i* names. The orthography of place names in Hawaiian is in accordance with the most recently revised edition of the Puku'i-Elbert-Mookini dictionary of *Place Names in Hawaii* (1974).

—Rubellite Kawena Johnson

# Acknowledgements

THERE ARE THREE GREAT SOURCES of information in this century about Hawaiian featherwork which describe in detail such facts as the size of the objects and garments, how they were made and where they may be seen today in the world's museums. In the great pioneering work of Dr. William T. Brigham, the first director of the Bernice Pauahi Bishop Museum, one learns much about where the feather articles came from and how they were acquired by the museum; and to the best of his ability he lists extant pieces of Hawaiian featherwork and their whereabouts. His first volume about Hawaiian featherwork was published by the Bernice Pauahi Bishop Museum in 1899. The second volume, #5, was released in 1903, and a third publication, *Additional Notes on Hawaiian Featherwork Second Supplement,* Volume VII, #1, was published in 1918.

In 1957, Sir Peter Buck published his *opus majoris, Arts and Crafts of Hawaii.* There is much to be learned in this book from his descriptions—particularly those concerning the making of old Hawaiian featherwork objects—and from drawings which illustrate various techniques used in applying feathers to the base netting of *'ōlona* fiber which was used in all feather constructions of old Hawai'i.

Meanwhile, a third source clearly tells us where old Hawaiian featherwork can be seen today, and to some extent reports how these articles were originally acquired (and where and when, whenever this is possible). These provenance writings, by Dr. Adrienne Kaeppler, are found in several publications. Since she was heavily involved in mounting the show at the Bernice Pauahi Bishop Museum in 1978 called *Artificial Curiosities,* and did much to locate items in the collections of various museums, she was selected to write the *Catalogue* for this exhibit. Many pieces of Hawaiian featherwork were seen in this exhibition, most appearing in Hawai'i for the first time.

In *Occasional Papers of the Bernice Pauahi Bishop Museum,* Vol XXIV, July 8, 1970, Dr. Kaeppler deals with the beginnings of ownership of well known garments after they left Hawai'i, some of which have been returned to Hawai'i and are now in the collection of the Bernice Pauahi Bishop Museum. She traces, for example, the acquisition of garments by the British gentlemen, Lord Elgin and The Earl of Kintore.

The third Kaeppler source of information about Hawaiian featherwork in world museums is titled *A Further Note of the Cook Voyage Collection in Leningrad,* Adrienne Kaeppler, Smithsonian Institution, from *The Journal of the Polynesian Society,* Volume 92, #1, March 1983. This invaluable work carefully traces from its acquisition at Kealakekua, and later Alaska, the Hawaiian feather collection now in the Leningrad Ethnographic Museum. It is an important source regarding many other pieces of featherwork which were collected during the visit of Captain James Cook.

I owe huge debt of gratitude to these three earlier toilers in the vineyard of Hawaiian ethnography and art who attempted to deal with the artistic, spiritual and philosophical aspects of Hawaiian featherwork art. Without the firm foundations they provide in telling us the where, how and when of Hawaiian featherwork objects one would be very weakly equipped to pursue a search for the meanings that underly these remarkable expressions of Hawaiian art. I express my gratitude to Dr. Brigham, Dr. Buck and to Dr. Kaeppler— *mai nei loko*—deep from the inside.

I also owe my deepest thanks to Dr. Roger Rose of the Ethnology Department of the Bernice Pauahi Bishop Museum, and to chief Librarian Cynthia Timberlake. Dr. Edward Creutz, former Director, made the museum's collections available to me and without this I could not have hoped to complete my work. Very special thanks is offered to Ben Patnoi, Museum photographer, who went to great pains to make it possible to photograph the *'ahuli'i* and *'ahu'ula* in the Museum's collection. My thanks also to Betty Long who assisted Ben Patnoi in performing the onerous task of carrying the museum's prized feather art pieces to and from the place they were being photographed and arranging them on the mannequins. Gratitude is also expressed for help received from the staff of the photographic archives of the Bernice Pauahi Bishop Museum. Also Dorota Starzeca, Grahma Leitch, John P. Hudson and other members of the British Museum staff for invaluable assistance. Thanks also to Dr. Hans Nammdorff, Dr. Hanns Peter, and Herr Mick of Museum für Völkerkunde Vienna, Austria, Madame Pattison of the Musse de l'Homme, Paris, Paul Mørk, Lisa Risøj Petersen and Bete'Due' of the Ethnographical Museum of Copenhagen, and Kersti Gustafsson of the Ethnographical Museum, Stockholm. I offer in the same spirit of gratitude my *aloha* to Sanna Deutsch and Hilde Randolph of the staff of the Honolulu Academy of Arts, and to Bob Chinn, photographer, whose special way of draping *lei hulu* on a mannequin is a refreshing new way of arranging feather *lei* to be photographed.

I must also offer special thanks to my assistant, Catherine Finlay Von Wiegandt, who traveled to Europe on a whirlwind tour to gather information and pictures about Hawaiian featherwork from various European museums. My thanks also to Denise deVone for the splendid illustrations which add a special quality to this book, Martha F. M. Smith for her advice and assistance, and to Hanakaulani Ferreira and Lyn Mauilani Holt for the hours spent in typing numerous drafts of this work. Also to Steve Shrader and Leonard Lueras, many thanks for helping in the organization and publication of this book. Thanks must also go to Nedra Lueras for her work on the index, to Grady Timmons and Jay Hartwell for help with the captioning and a special thanks to Rubellite Kawena Johnson for help in the spelling and punctuation of Hawaiian words. And finally to my wife Patches Damon Holt, a special thanks for her assistance.

Finally I wish to express my gratitude to the Directors of the Hawaii Cultural Research Foundation for making a grant to begin this work.

—J.D.H.

# Index

# Bibliography

J. C. Beaglehole, Editor, *The Journals of Captain James Cook,* London, 1967.

Berger, Andrew, *Hawaiian Birdlife,* University of Hawaii Press,

Brigham, William T., *Additional Notes on Hawaiian Featherwork,* Second Supplement, Volume VII, #1, Bernice Pauahi Bishop Museum, Honolulu, 1918.

Buck, Sir Peter, *Arts and Crafts of Hawaii,* Bernice Pauahi Bishop Museum, Honolulu, 1957.

Force, R. W. and Force, M., *Art and Artifacts of the 18th Century,* Bernice Pauahi Bishop Museum, Honolulu, 1968.

Kaeppler, Adrienne, *Artificial Curiosities,* Bernice Pauahi Bishop Museum, 1978.

Kaeppler, Adrienne, *A Further Note of the Cook Voyage Collection in Leningrad,* Smithsonian Institution, The Journal of the Polynesian Society, Volume 92, #1, 1983.

Pukui, M. K., and Elbert, S. H., *Hawaiian Dictionary,* University Press of Hawaii, Honolulu, 1971.

Rose, Roger G., *Symbols of Sovereignty, Feather Girdles of Tahiti and Hawaii,* Department of Anthropology, Bernice Pauahi Bishop Museum, Honolulu, 1978.

# Art Credits

Ben Patnoi, Bernice Pauahi Bishop Museum photographer
Seth Joel, Bernice Pauahi Bishop Museum photographer
Bob Chinn, Honolulu Academy of Arts photographer
Denise De Vone, illustrations
George Bacon, photographer, Honolulu
National Ethnographic Museum, Copenhagen
W. Rothschild, Lithographs, Avifauna of Laysan
and the Adjacent Islands, 1893 –1900
Wilson and Evans, Lithographs, Birds of the
Sandwich Islands, 1890 –1899
The Peabody Museum, Cambridge
Mr. & Mrs. Donald Woodrum, Honolulu
Hawai'i State Archives, Honolulu
The British Museum, London